DANGLING NOOSE

When Dan Chantry, a struggling farmer, is threatened with foreclosure, a meeting between him and Morgan, his unsympathetic bank manager, turns angry. Chantry vows to stop him should Morgan carry out his threat. Then Morgan is found murdered, and the murder weapon is found in Chantry's saddlebag. His next stop is the gallows. However he escapes imprisonment, but Al Blake, a friend and marshal of Wolf Creek, captures him. Will Chantry be proved innocent or will he face the gallows?

Books by Jack Holt
in the Linford Western Library:

GUNHAWK'S REVENGE
PETTICOAT MARSHAL
HOT LEAD RANGE
HARD RIDE TO LARGO

JACK HOLT

DANGLING NOOSE

Complete and Unabridged

LINFORD
Leicester

First published in Great Britain in 2007 by
Robert Hale Limited
London

First Linford Edition
published 2008
by arrangement with
Robert Hale Limited
London

British Library CIP Data

Holt, Jack
   Dangling noose.—Large print ed.—
Linford western library
1. Western stories
2. Large type books
I. Title
823.9'2 [F]

ISBN 978–1–84782–241–3

Published by
F. A. Thorpe (Publishing)
Anstey, Leicestershire

Set by Words & Graphics Ltd.
Anstey, Leicestershire
Printed and bound in Great Britain by
T. J. International Ltd., Padstow, Cornwall

This book is printed on acid-free paper

1

'I'm doing the best I know how, Mr Morgan.' Charles B. Morgan, the president of the Wolf Creek bank shrugged, unimpressed by Dan Chantry's earnest statement. 'Come harvest time — '

'We've had two previous harvests, Chantry,' Morgan interjected unsympathetically. 'It made no difference. Fact is, this is not crop-growing country.'

'Last couple of years were pretty dry, sure,' Chantry conceded. 'But the rains must come — '

'No must about it, Chantry!' Morgan barked.

'By the fall I expect to be able to pay what I owe,' Chantry said, trying to ignore the banker's dismissive and belittling attitude.

'I've got the bank to think of, Chantry. You owe all over town. Get in first and I just might get my hands on some of what's owed the bank. Should never have given you a loan on that dustbowl you call a farm to begin with.'

Charles B. Morgan held up his hand to stay the farmer's pleading.

'If you have to meet all your debts in full everyone will get peanuts. By foreclosing now, I'll be at the head of the queue.'

'I've fattened the coffers of this bank in the good times.' There was anger now in Dan Chantry's voice. 'I've broken my back retrieving acres from the desert to make my farm at least ten times more valuable than when you gave me a mortgage, Morgan. If you foreclose now all that sweat and labour will count for nought.' Chantry's grey eyes glinted with anger. 'I reckon that ain't even near fair!'

Morgan was unmoved.

'It's nothing personal, Chantry,' he said, hunching his expensively clad, well-beefed shoulders. 'It's just business. You knew how it would be if you defaulted.'

'I'll pay the bank every cent.'

'Sure you will, but when? Your payments are already way overdue.'

'Like I said, when — '

'I know, when that bumper harvest will come in,' the banker interjected derisively. 'I'm only interested in the here and now, Chantry,' he barked. 'Promises have no cash value.'

The bank president glared at Chantry. 'Now, can you put dollars on the table or not?'

'You know I can't!'

'Then . . . ' Morgan again hunched his shoulders. 'But I'm not an unreasonable man. Say a week to quit your holding.'

Dan Chantry sprang off the chair he was sitting on, stormed to the office door and yanked it open. 'I've worked too damn hard, banker, to let you grab what's rightly mine. I'll see you in hell before I'll yield up an inch of my land.'

As he stormed out of the Wolf Creek bank, Dan Chantry was conscious of eyes on him, and he could hear the teller ask, 'Are you OK, Mr Morgan? That Chantry is mad enough to kill.'

'Get on with your work, Beecham,' Morgan bellowed from his office.

'Yes, Mr Morgan, sir.'

'Heh, teller, this is a one-dollar bill you gave me, not a ten,' complained the customer the teller was dealing with.

Andy Beecham became flustered. 'Sorry, Mr Clinton,' he apologized. 'As you can see, I'm not wearing my usual specs, broke them. These specs I'm wearing are old. Can't see very well with them. Have new ones soon.'

'Meantime, I'll be a poor man, Beecham!' Clinton growled. 'Be sure to count every cent,' he advised the other customers waiting.

Charging out of the bank unheedingly, Chantry bumped into Al Blake, the marshal of Wolf Creek, with such force that the big man staggered back and had to grab the hitch rail to avoid falling on his backside in the street.

'Got a bee in your drawers, Dan?' he asked, when back on his feet.

'Shouldn't that be bonnet?' Chantry flung back.

'It would, if you were wearing a bonnet,' the marshal returned with equal snappiness.

Chantry groaned. 'Sorry, Al. I should have looked where I was going.'

'He threatened Mr Morgan, Marshal,' the sly Andy Beecham whined. 'I feared for Mr Morgan's life and limb just now.'

'What's he talking about, Dan?' Al Blake questioned the farmer, closely.

Beecham would not be denied his big moment. 'Said he'd see Mr Morgan in hell before he'd let him take an inch of his land, Marshal.'

'Shuddup, Andy!' Blake barked. 'Dan . . . ?'

'It's as he says, Al,' Dan Chantry admitted. 'And I mean every damn word, too.'

'What are you going to do about it, Marshal?' the sneaky bank-teller pressed Al Blake. 'We' — his hand swept the bank's interior — 'all heard

5

Chantry threaten Mr Morgan.'

'My teller has asked a good question, Marshal Blake.' Attention focused on Charles B. Morgan as he appeared in the bank doorway. 'I'm an important citizen,' he said pompously. 'In fact Wolf Creek's most important, I'd venture to claim. Am I to be insulted by a mere dirt-farmer, Marshal?'

'Everyone is equal in law, Mr Morgan,' Blake said, his steely glare expressing his ire at being handed a public reprimand. He turned to Dan Chantry. 'What have you got to say, Dan?'

'Nothing more,' was Chantry's tetchy response.

'Are you still holding to your threat?' Blake asked, surprised and annoyed that Dan Chantry had not taken the opportunity to apologize to Morgan and take the problem off his plate. 'Threatening a citizen, any citizen, is a serious offence.'

'It wasn't a threat, Marshal Blake,' Chantry said. Thinking that Chantry was suing for peace, the Wolf Creek lawman smiled broadly and looked to Morgan to match Chantry's first step towards the restoration of harmonious relations. However, when Dan Chantry spoke again, he was stunned. 'It was a promise,' he stated bluntly.

He turned to glare at Charles B. Morgan.

'If you or any of your agents come anywhere near my property, I'll drop you on sight, Morgan!'

So intense was Dan Chantry's anger that the banker withdrew into the shadows of the bank. 'The man is as crazy as a rabid dog, can't you see that, Marshal?'

'OK,' Al Blake said regretfully. 'You know where the jail is, Chantry.'

Dan Chantry bristled at Charles B. Morgan's smug chuckle.

'Like I said, Morgan, if you come anyway near my land I'll — '

'That's enough, Chantry!' the Wolf Creek marshal barked. 'Now start walking!'

As they marched along to the jail, Blake said, 'If you grind your teeth any more you'll break your jaw, Dan.'

'Or bust yours!' Chantry flung back.

'You could darn well try,' Blake returned, with equal acrimony.

'Why the hell are you slinging me in jail, Al?' Chantry groused. 'Morgan's the crook.'

'It won't be for long,' the marshal assured Chantry. 'A couple of hours, I'll jaw with Morgan and you can go home then.'

'I don't want any favours,' Chantry shot back.

'You know, Dan Chantry,' Blake said, teeth now as gritted as the farmer's, 'I've known you since we rolled into town in those battered wagons all those years ago, and I swear that you've got more contrary by the day. Don't you know better than to give sass to a fella like Charles B. Morgan. He owns this town.'

'Maybe that's what's wrong with this town,' Chantry grumbled, turning into the marshal's office. He spun round to face Blake. 'This used to be a town where folk helped each other, and where the small and struggling man could count on his neighbours to pitch in when he needed help. Now fellas like Morgan hold sway over everything and everyone. And it looks like the law is slanted towards looking after the interests of these well-heeled gents by slinging in jail anyone who disagrees with the way they're running this burg.'

Al Blake's temper flared.

'Are you saying that I'm crooked, Dan?' he challenged Chantry. ''Cause if you are, so help me, I'll strap a gun on your hip and call you out!'

The steam suddenly went out of Chantry.

'You know better than that, Al. You've always brought honour to your badge. But you do understand how things are going wrong round here, don't you?'

Marshal Al Blake nodded.

'I know you're right, Dan,' he conceded, heavy-shouldered. 'So much so that pretty soon I'll be moving on.'

Chantry was stunned.

'Moving on? This town needs good men, Al. Men who'll again make it the kind of town it used to be,' Chantry pleaded.

Blake shook his head regretfully.

'The town's gone bad, Dan. And when a town goes bad, in my opinion, there's no way to turn back the damn clock. Anyway,' he flung his hands in the air in despair, 'times are a-changing all over the West. Ain't what it used to be.' He scoffed. 'They call it progress, Dan.'

'In a pig's eye!' Chantry growled.

'Face it, Dan,' Al Blake said, 'our time is over. The railroad will be here in another year and this town will turn more and more to commerce and more and more away from farming and ranching — especially sodbusting.'

'So you're just going to walk away,' Chantry challenged, a clear note of disappointment in his voice. 'The Al Blake I used to know wouldn't have done that.'

The Wolf Creek marshal looked at his old friend with a weary sadness.

'That Al Blake has got a lot older, Dan. My sister Amy has settled back East. She says that I should stop eating all this dust and join her and her husband. He owns a couple of hardware stores. Amy says that John will see me right. Give me a job in one of his stores.'

Dan Chantry shook his head in disbelief.

'Al Blake, clerking!' he exclaimed. 'Never thought I'd live to see the day.'

'Clerking nine to five, instead of busting drunks and ornery critters like you all hours of day and night ain't too bad to my way of thinking.'

Dan Chantry studied his old friend.

'John Bascombe is a very influential man, Dan,' the marshal continued. 'I reckon, if we arrived on his doorstep together, he'd have you fixed up in no time at all.'

'I'm a Westerner, Al,' Chantry intoned. 'I like the smell of the earth. The changing of the seasons. The soft summer breezes and the colder winter winds coming off the mountains. What the hell would I be doing back East?'

'Living a civilized life,' Blake suggested.

'Dying a torturous death, more likely.'

'Why do you go on breaking your back trying to grow crops in soil that God never intended crops to grow in, Dan?'

Dan Chantry grinned.

'I guess maybe I'm a touch loco, Al.'

'Only one thing I'll miss about this place,' Blake said, his eyes reflecting his memories. 'And that is that I'll be leaving Mary behind, all alone.'

Chantry followed the marshal's gaze to the cemetery on a slope overlooking the town.

'Mary will never be alone while I'm around,' he promised. 'I'll drop by regularly to chat, Al. And to read those letters you'll be sending me from back East.'

'That's good to hear, Dan,' the marshal said soulfully. 'You know, Mary could have tied the knot with you instead of me.' He chuckled. 'It's just that I was so much better-looking.'

Dan Chantry let it go. He had never told his old friend that had he been prepared to give up farming and take the marshal's badge that was on offer at the time. Mary Fitzgerald, all the way from County Galway, would have been Mrs Dan Chantry instead of Mrs Al Blake. Mary had left a dirt-poor farm behind her in Galway. 'And I'll be damned if I'm going to ever try again to get crops to grow on land that the only difference between it and the land in Galway, is that Galway's got rock while this darn place has sand, Dan,' she'd said.

'Me toting a badge could make you an early widow,' Chantry had argued.

Mary had turned to him, her face openly honest, the wind catching her red hair and blowing it across her face.

'At least, Dan, I wouldn't be burying you with a humped back and gnarled hands, like I did my father,' she had said. 'And as dirt-poor as the land he had slaved to conquer, too.'

The next day Al Blake, with whom Dan had been in contention with for Mary's hand, had come riding helter-skeleter into his yard. 'Dan, I need me a best man,' he'd hollered, leaping from the saddle and running with his horse. 'Mary's accepted my proposal, on the thousandth invite.'

Bereft, Dan had almost ridden into town and told Mary Fitzgerald that he would do as she wanted. However, that would ruin his best friend's happiness. And maybe Mary would reject him anyway, now that she had decided on Al Blake. She was an honourable woman and probably would, though love sometimes changed a person's long-held values. He had decided against, never sure that he had done so in Al's and Mary's best interests. Or his own fear of rejection.

'The wedding's in two days,' Al had said. 'Have you got anything near decent to wear?'

'What I've got is what I'm standing up in, Al,' Chantry had said with false cheeriness.

'You got soap?' Al had asked fearfully.

'Soap I've got.'

'Well, at least you'll smell nice, I guess. I'd buy you a suit, but I ain't got the shekels, Dan.'

'You and me both, friend,' Chantry had replied.

'You know, Dan, that Mary could have taken either one of us as a husband. I just happened to have a lucky edge over you, that's all.'

'You treat Mary well, Al,' Chantry said. 'Or I'll whup you good and proper.'

'I'll treat her like a darn queen, friend,' Blake had promised. And Al Blake had lived up to that promise and more. Now, after all the years, the Wolf Creek marshal confessed, 'I've always known that I was second best to you, Dan.'

15

'Don't talk horse manure,' Chantry protested. 'Mary loved you, Al. That's why she married you, darn it.'

'Ain't true. Oh, Mary loved me all right, but not as much as she loved you, Dan. I never could understand why you let her go, for all the acres in New Mexico.' And in response to Dan Chantry's dropping jaw, he explained, 'Mary never knew 'cause I never told her. But, you see, Dan, she talked in her sleep, and it sure was hard listening to her mention your name in a way that tore the heart right out of me.

'But come morning, she'd look at me, and I knew that whatever she thought about you, she'd always be mine because that was the choice she had made.'

Al Blake looked curiously at Dan Chantry.

'How come you didn't ride into town and take her from me that day I rode out to the farm to tell you that Mary had accepted my proposal, Dan? You could have. I couldn't understand that

16

far-off look you had that day, until that first night Mary talked in her sleep. Then I understood.'

'Because I guess I was scared,' Chantry admitted.

'Scared?'

'That my pride would be dented if she stuck with you, Al. And then, later, when I saw you two as close as doves in a nest, I reckoned that I'd been wise to keep my mouth shut that day.'

Al Blake slumped wearily in the chair behind his desk.

'You know, Chantry,' he said, his laughter hollow, 'we're two of the dumbest critters that ever came down the line.'

'Well, hindsight's a great giver of wisdom, Al. But the thing is that it's always too darn late when it delivers it.'

'Git!' the marshal said.

'You're not going to sling me in jail? What about Charles B. Morgan?'

'Charles B. Morgan can go jump in the lake!' Blake declared.

17

'We haven't got a lake round here, Al.'

'You'll go to the grave smart-mouthing, won't you, Chantry.'

Dan Chantry's smile was broad.

'Go eat some more dust, sodbuster,' Al Blake said, good-naturedly.

When Dan Chantry left, Blake said, 'Did you hear that, Mary? You should have married a man like Charles B. Morgan instead of a poor as a church mouse badge-toter.' The hind legs of the chair he was leaning back on slipped and he crashed to the floor. He laughed. 'Always had a temper to match that red Irish head of yours, didn't you!'

As Chantry left the marshal's office, Andy Beecham, the bank-teller, was at the bank door. On seeing Chantry free as a bird, he dived back into the bank, no doubt to alert his employer. By the time Chantry was half-way along the board-walk to his horse hitched to the rail outside the bank, Morgan had joined the teller at the bank door.

'And where do you think you're

going, Chantry?' the banker questioned.

'Home,' Chantry answered bluntly. 'And you're not invited, Morgan.'

As he swung his horse, Morgan was bearing down on the marshal's office, every inch of his rotund figure bristling with indignation.

'Mr Morgan is going to kick you off your land, sodbuster.' The weasel bank-teller sniggered.

'Try, and he'll be buried on it!' Chantry vowed.

2

Al Blake looked up at Morgan as he stormed in.

'Marshal,' he barked angrily.

'I don't want to hear it, Morgan,' Blake growled. 'Dan Chantry committed no crime, except to give you lip you well deserve.'

Charles B. Morgan went purple in the face.

'I'll call an immediate meeting of the town council and have your badge, Blake,' he fumed.

'The door's behind you,' Blake barked, his anger matching Morgan's.

The purple of the banker's face became livid, but Al Blake could not care less. Dan Chantry was right, Wolf Creek had lost its homely charm, spirited away by men like Charles B. Morgan whose only reason for living was to pile more dollars on top of the stack they had already accumulated by mostly chicanery and underhanded dealings.

'You can't talk that way to Mr Morgan.' Andy Beecham entered the marshal's office behind his employer, sucking up as usual.

'This town is getting more and more vermin all the time,' Blake said, his contempt for the bank-teller total.

'Who's minding the bank, Beecham?' Morgan bellowed.

'No one,' the teller whined, cowering. The banker staggered and the purple of his face was washed away by a tide of pallor. 'It's OK, sir,' Beecham's whine increased tenfold, 'I locked up.'

'A locked bank doesn't make any money, you fool!' Morgan roared. 'Open for business this instant.'

'I thought — '

'You're not paid to think,' Morgan sneered. 'And I'll want to see you at close of business, Beecham. We've got things to talk about.'

Andy Beecham blanched. 'Have we,

sir, Mr Morgan?' His gaze became shifty. 'What would that be, sir?'

'You'll find out,' the banker said, his eyes boring through his teller.

Al Blake chuckled at Beecham's sidling retreat.

'Now, Marshal,' Charles B. Morgan returned his full attention and glare to Al Blake, 'I think you should ride out to Chantry's place right now and haul him back to jail. And before you leave, I demand an apology.'

'Go stick your head in cow-dung, Morgan,' the Wolf Creek lawman glowered.

★ ★ ★

The ride back to his farm was taken at a leisurely pace, Dan Chantry taking time to relish the invigorating breeze from the mountains to the south of his farm. His anxiety for rain might be putting a false scent in his nostrils, but he reckoned that for the first time in a long time, the wind bore rain on it.

He had a great deal to ponder on, Al Blake's impending departure from Wolf Creek being high on his list of thoughts. Over the years most of the men he had arrived in town with as part of a wagon train had died or had already moved on, once the rigours of trying to ranch or farm the unyielding soil wore them down. Their passing or departure was keenly felt, as good friends drifted away or went to their Maker. And some had been forced out by leeches like Charles B. Morgan. But he had never thought that Al Blake would join the exodus. He had thought that even Al's daily pilgrimage to Mary's grave would be enough to keep him put until the day he joined her in the hereafter. However, Mary's death had affected Al greatly, and his once jilty mood had slowly ebbed away to be replaced by a dourness bordering on bitterness. Maybe, Chantry thought, it might be best if the marshal did go East and start anew. And maybe he should do the same. Not go East, he'd detest city living, but perhaps to some place where the earth was rich and yielding. If truth be told, he had only farmed the barren soil as he had done because his stubborn streak would not allow him to countenance failure. If he decided to leave, unencumbered by a wife or family, with belongings that were not worth taking along, his move would be an easy one. Any time he wanted to, he could saddle up and ride away. And now that Al Blake would no longer be around Wolf Creek, it was something he would give a whole lot of thought to.

By the time Dan reached the farm, Charles B. Morgan was about to chair an emergency meeting of the Wolf Creek Town Council. The banker had just called the meeting to order when Al Blake entered the back room of the general store where the meeting was being held and threw his badge on the floor. Without speaking, he turned and walked out again.

'Well, that saves us kicking him out,' Morgan gloated.

'Where are we going to get another marshal of Al Blake's stature?' one dissenting voice asked, the voice of Lou Rawlings, the undertaker, and the only man on the town council who did not owe Morgan a dime.

'There'll be plenty of candidates, I'm sure,' the banker said, starchily dismissing Rawlings' concerns.

'I don't doubt that, Morgan,' Rawlings piped up. 'But it's quality and not quantity that counts.' Rawlings's gaze flashed across the other five men present. 'Ain't anyone else got anything to say?' Eyes were averted, and heads went down. 'This town can ill-afford to lose a good man like Al Blake,' the undertaker added.

'Now,' Charles B. Morgan pressed on, ignoring, like everyone else present, the undertaker's protest, 'the first task for the new marshal, whom we should appoint right away, will be to arrest Dan Chantry for threatening behaviour.'

'Who did he threaten?' Rawlings asked, and added instantly on seeing the puff of the banker's chest, 'That was a horse's-ass of a question. Is it true that you're going to foreclose on Chantry, Morgan?'

'That is my intention,' the banker confirmed stiffly.

'I know Dan Chantry like the back of my hand,' Rawlings said. 'No question, he'll pay you every dime owing.'

'It's been owing for too long,' Morgan barked.

'Without rain you can't grow crops,' Rawlings said. 'But the rains can't take forever to come. Chantry's first good harvest will clear his debt.'

'Banks and bankers can't wait for rain, Rawlings.'

'Can't?' the undertaker questioned sourly. 'Don't you mean won't, Morgan?'

Charles B. Morgan turned his face against Rawlings and addressed the other members of the council who were taking note of his exchange and were anxious that the banker would not do to them what he had done to Dan Chantry.

'All in favour of accepting Marshal

Blake's resignation,' he said.

Lou Rawlings's was the only hand that stayed down.

'Motion carried,' Morgan cried out, his smug gaze fixed on the undertaker, knowing that any challenge offered by him would most assuredly be defeated. 'Now I propose that we post the marshal's vacancy immediately on the town billboard.'

Rawlings's hand was again the only one to remain down. Charles B. Morgan preened himself.

'I think that concludes the business of this meeting, gentlemen,' the banker announced triumphantly. 'Thank you for your prompt attendance, gents. If you will excuse me, I have other urgent business to attend to.'

Andy Beecham, the bank-teller, jumped when Morgan entered his office, where he had been nervously waiting since he had closed the bank an hour before. Morgan went behind his desk, sat, let Beecham sweat for a while longer, enjoying his teller's distress before he eventually said, 'Now, Beecham, I've been going through the books . . . '

★   ★   ★

Dan Chantry woke to the light of a full moon, unsure of what had disturbed his sleep. A bucket clattered across the yard, driven by a wind that had blown up. Chantry thought about the rain that might accompany the wind but did not get excited, he'd been waiting too long for the rains to come for that.

He turned over and went back to sleep.

Later, the first greys of dawn were streaking the sky when he woke again. A storm was howling and to his delight he heard the sound of rain on the cabin roof. But he reckoned that it was not the storm that had woken him, but the clomp of horses in the yard.

Close to the border, the arrival of unexpected riders was always a concern.

He could tell that there were at least

three riders. His patch of New Mexico was on a much-travelled outlaw route. Most times the hardcases would ride harmlessly by, intent only on seeking refuge across the border. A couple of times men not so pushed had stopped by but, on investigation, had had more pity for his impoverished existence than any malice and had quickly moved on, pausing only to fill their canteens if there was enough water in the well.

The mountains to the south of the farm had many trails that led to the border, particularly one called the Fatbelly Trail, the quickest and most favoured outlaw escape route. His knowledge of the mountains was more learned than experienced. Having devoted every waking hour trying to coax the soil, he had not travelled far from a plough, only to where he needed to go and that was mostly to town.

Chantry leapt out of bed and was in the main room of the cabin reaching for a rifle when the cabin door was kicked in and Al Blake, backed by another man from town, sixguns cocked, filled the open door. A third man, Willie Acton, a town layabout, came running soaked through by the rains that had come at last.

'Found this, Marshal,' he said. Chantry looked in alarm at the bloodstained hunting-knife which Acton was waving above his head. 'In Chantry's saddle-bag.'

'You're under arrest for the murder of Charles B. Morgan, Dan,' Al Blake declared, with as weary a breath as he had ever drawn.

3

'That ain't my knife, Al,' Dan Chantry said.

'It was in your saddle-bag,' Blake responded, gruffly.

'Then someone put it there,' Chantry replied with equal gruffness.

'Likely yarn,' Willie Acton said. 'You gutted Mr Morgan with this knife.' He flourished the wicked blade.

'Gutted Morgan,' he exclaimed, shocked. 'I haven't been anywhere near town!'

'You said you'd kill Morgan, and you did,' Acton snarled.

'I said I'd kill him if he tried to take my land, and I meant it, too. But I did not murder Charles B. Morgan. I swear I didn't, Al.'

'It's kind of hard to believe that you did,' the Wolf Creek marshal conceded. 'But how do you explain how this knife got in your saddle-bag, Dan?'

31

'Obviously, the killer put it there. He knew of my threat to Morgan and grabbed his opportunity to murder the banker and have me hang for it.

'I'd like to believe you, Dan,' Blake said. 'But as the marshal, I've got to act on the evidence.' He shook his head. 'Yesterday, Morgan called a meeting of the town council to kick me out. I beat him to the punch and resigned.'

'Resigned? So strictly speaking you're not the marshal of Wolf Creek?'

'No. But until a new marshal is appointed, I figured that I had a duty, bitter as it is, to step in until another marshal is appointed by the town council later today.'

'I'll hogtie him, Al,' Acton volunteered, stepping forward with a length of rope.

'No need for that, Acton,' Blake growled.

'It ain't my knife, Al,' Dan Chantry repeated.

'I've also got a witness, Dan.'

'A witness?' Chantry exclaimed,

stunned by Blake's revelation.

'Andy Beecham. Says he saw you skulking around Morgan's house around midnight.'

'He's a liar!'

'Beecham says he couldn't sleep. Thought the night air might help. Went for a stroll.'

'Well, the man he saw wasn't me, Al,' Dan Chantry stated. 'And if I was skulking, as Beecham says, why didn't he do something about it? Like telling you, Al.'

'Beecham says that he didn't want to wake me. And that, having thrown in my badge, I wasn't the law any more.'

'Beecham's story is a mossy one, Al.'

'You'll have a chance to say your piece in court, Dan,' Blake said. 'This storm is working up spite. Let's make tracks for town before creeks and gullies flood, if they already haven't.'

Marshal Al Blake forlornly looked at Dan Chantry and shook his head.

'You're a dumb critter, Dan. Killing

33

Morgan, just when the rains have come.'

'How many times do I have to tell you, Al,' Chantry said angrily. 'I didn't murder Charles B. Morgan.'

The first streaks of lightning raced along ahead of them as they rode out of Chantry's yard, and the rain became a virtual waterfall.

'You've got your rains, Dan,' Blake observed sombrely.

'It's too damn heavy,' Chantry said. 'It'll just run off.'

'Nothing much is going right for you, Dan,' Blake said sympathetically. 'Maybe we both should have quit this burg a long time ago.'

'Right now, Al,' Chantry said, 'that makes a whole mountain of sense, my friend.'

A sudden, blinding fork of lightning split the heavens open and came to earth with scorching spite. It split a tree just ahead and it crashed down, aflame. A branch of the tree side-swiped the leading rider and smashed him to the

34

ground. The heavenly violence spooked Acton's horse and the rearing stallion threw him. He fell heavily and lay winded, moaning.

Taking advanatage of nature's intervention, Dan Chantry swung a pile-driver to the side of Blake's head that lifted him out of his saddle. Then he galloped away.

'I'll be back to clear my name, Al,' he called back.

The Wolf Creek marshal got off a reaction shot at his fleeing prisoner but, because he was unbalanced, his bullet went harmlessly wide of its target.

As Dan Chantry ate up trail, he wondered about where he was going and when he would be coming back, if ever. He was an innocent man, but as far as the law was concerned he was a fugitive from justice and would become fair game for any lawman or bounty hunter who got him in his gun-sights. Where could he go? Mexico was the nearest hideout. The Rio Grande would act as a barrier between him and US lawmen. However, the Rio would not protect him from bounty hunters, because they did not have to worry about their official standing, as a US lawman would. And what of Al Blake? Would he give chase to his oldest friend? As of now he was a prisoner who had got away from Blake's custody and, from long experience, Dan Chantry knew that once Blake took on a job he became dogged about seeing it through. But, by Al Blake's own admission, he had handed in his badge and had only acted until a new marshal was appointed. Might he take back his badge long enough to bring his last prisoner to justice? Blake would hate to quit with a blemish on his proud record. And if he did quit, it would leave him free of his official standing as a US lawman to cross into Mexico to seek him out. But did he have to go to Mexico? Dan thought of Herb Gentry, an old friend from the war, who had started a horse ranch within spitting distance of the Mexican border.

'Mex breeding stock is about the best

there is,' he had told Dan four years previously when he was passing through Wolf Creek on a journey to fulfil his long-time dream of breeding the best horses in the West. 'You come visit some time.' He had looked around at the dusty fields. 'Maybe you should ride with me now, Dan. Crops and dust don't make a good partnership, friend. Together, we could build the finest breeding stock in the whole darn West.'

Hindsight had proved Herb Gentry right. But when Gentry had made his more than generous offer, he had made it at a time when Dan Chantry's pride was at stake and his determination not to fail had been at its most stubborn.

Later, he learned from a rider passing through Wolf Creek, whose horse Dan had admired, that Herb Gentry had been as good as his word.

'Got this stallion from a fella by the name of Herb Gentry down near the border,' the rider had told Chantry, proudly boastful of the fine animal. 'Breeds the best darn horseflesh in these parts and any other parts too, I reckon.'

Dan Chantry knew that Herb Gentry would not hesitate to give him shelter until he could work out a plan to clear his name, but would it be fair to load his troubles on Herb?

Seeking refuge with Herb Gentry would have the advantage of being an American in America, and consequently hiding out would be easier. Were he to cross the Rio, he'd be an *Americano* in Mexico and would attract attention — probably the wrong kind, too. Because other than traders who crossed the border to trade, the only other Americans who crossed into Mexico were, for the most part, men who needed to vanish for a spell to let things Stateside cool down; men who were in the main cut-throats forced to associate with cut-throats to survive.

Dan Chantry decided that he would make for Herb Gentry's ranch. There, while he worked for his keep, he would devise a plan to restore his good name and save his neck from a hangman's noose. Recalling that Gentry was a man who watched his pennies, he would not refuse an offer of labour for grub.

He swung by a neighbour to buy what meagre rations he could from him, before cutting through the mountains to link up with the Fatbelly Trail.

'What in tarnation's happened, Dan, that's got you all fired up?' his neighbour sleepily enquired when Chantry pressed on him his need to not dally and to burn up trail.

'Ain't got time to jaw, Frank,' he'd said. 'You'll hear the story soon enough.'

After putting the little that Frank Lawton could spare into his saddle-bags, Chantry headed into the mountains to seek out the Fatbelly Trail, the quickest route to the border.

'Ain't headin' into the mountains in this downpour, are ya?' Lawton asked, when Dan swung his horse, leaving only one way to go. 'Someone knock the sense out of your skull? Those hills will be like raging torrents, Dan.'

'Thanks for the help, Frank,' Chantry said and rode away, leaving Lawton scratching his head.

'What is it, Frank?' Freda Lawton enquired, coming from the bedroom.

'It's Dan Chantry, honey,' he answered. 'Looks like he's gone loco.'

Lawton was right, the downpour would not help. Chantry saw the bitter irony of his situation. He had waited patiently for rain to come, and now that it had, its arrival would work against him every bit as much as its absence had previously. Another worry was his topographical ignorance of the mountains, which would at best slow his progress and could, if his lousy luck did not break, have him roaming aimlessly through the mountains looking for the elusive Fatbelly Trail.

'Findin' the Fatbelly, if you don't know how, is down to pure luck.'

Recalling the words of a US marshal who had stopped by one day to refresh

40

himself, sent Chantry's spirits plum-meting. Because he did not have the know-how, and he was flush out of luck.

Dan Chantry had no doubt that the lawman in Al Blake would not rest until his last prisoner was back safely in his custody, even if that fugitive was a friend.

Though Blake might believe that he was innocent, the marshal would still stick to the principles that had made him an honest and fair-minded badge-toter, and he would leave the question of Chantry's guilt for a judge and jury to decide. It was a much admired code of honour, which had served Wolf Creek and its citizens well, and Chantry could have no quibble with it because, over the years he too had been a beneficiary of Blake's honesty.

The blame for his predicament rested squarely with Andy Beecham, the bank-teller, who had given false witness against him. But to prove that he had would be Chantry's task, if ever the

41

opportunity or means presented themselves. That was some time in the future. His only course of action now was to put distance between himself and Al Blake, and hope to clear his name later.

Dan Chantry's other concern was his lack of riding skills. As a sodbuster he had spent more time behind nags than on them. Many of the mountain trails were narrow and treacherous, skirting dangerous gullies and ravines, and from the description he had heard of the Fatbelly Trail it was the trickiest to negotiate of the lot, parts of it barely wide enough for a single rider.

With a heart as heavy as stone, Dan Chantry rode up the slopes, wondering when he would be able to return, and how he could prove his innocence.

4

The higher he climbed into the mountains, the more keen Chantry's worry became. The storm had run its course, but the downpour on soil that had not seen rain for a long time made the underfoot conditions treacherous. Already there had been several occasions on which he had just been in time to stop the mare's slide on the soft, glutinous earth. Logging had stripped stretches of the mountains, leaving the soil thin and powdery; too thin for firm purchase, but plentiful enough to hide dangerous shale and sharp stones that would injure a horse. These bare stretches would also expose him to view, and had to be crossed quickly, thereby increasing the risk of mishap. In parts thick scrub had sprung up which also held a threat in the hidden roots and stumps of felled trees, some hacked down rather than cut cleanly, leaving behind spiked remains as sharp as a hunting-blade that could, if unlucky, maim man or beast as surely and as deadly as a real blade.

Growing increasingly frustrated with his slow progress, Chantry drew rein and let his eyes scan the mountains in the forlorn hope of seeing a clear path to where he wanted to get to. But no flash of insight was forthcoming. Trail snaked into trail and hill into hill with, seemingly, no beginning or end. Where his knowledge was lacking, the Wolf Creek marshal's would be excellent. And where his horsemanship was adequate, Al Blake's would be superb. Blake would know the short cuts, and he would ride the mountain trails with the same ease as he would the main street in Wolf Creek.

Weary of spirit, Dan Chantry realised the mammoth task he would have to beat Al Blake to the border, unless Blake figured that he had taken the direct and regular route. His hope of that happening was brief. Blake would read his mind, the way longtime friends could. On starting out he had thought that taking the mountain route to the border was the clever option, whereas, in effect, it was probably the dumbest thing he could have done.

All he had going for him was dogged determination to one day return and clear his name, but determination might not be enough to give him the breathing space he'd need to make that happen.

As he climbed, the colder air of the higher ground began to pinch. Not clad to deal with the chilly atmosphere, Chantry found himself huddling lower and lower in the saddle against the stiff breeze which had blown up, pressing his soaked clothing against him to chill him further.

He drew rein often to set in his mind the topography of the mountains which, disturbingly, were becoming more and more alike the higher he climbed, rise merging seamlessly into rise until any distinguishing landmarks he had noted lost their certainty.

He had heard tell of men who had become lost and had wandered around the mountains until their minds gave out. Now, glancing round him, on his latest stop to try and make sense of his surroundings, Dan Chantry could well understand how stories that seemed so much hooey down on the plains, up in the mountains had a stark and frightening reality.

If there was any consolation to be found, it was his total solitude. From his eagle's perch he had a bird's eye view of the slopes below him, and he saw no sign of pursuit. But unless he got the lucky break he needed, the mountains would achieve what the hangman would have done.

5

'You can't hand in your badge now, Al,' pleaded Arthur Bell, Charles B. Morgan's replacement as the chairman of the Wolf Creek town council. 'Not before Dan Chantry is brought to book for Morgan's murder. By the time we appoint another marshal, if anyone will take the darn job, that is, Chantry will be long gone.'

The Wolf Creek marshal understood the reasonableness of Bell's appeal, and since he had returned to town he had been trying to decide whether his decision to quit was because he had already chosen to do so, or because by resigning his badge he would not be faced with the harsh task of hunting down Dan Chantry, his oldest and dearest friend.

'Murder is murder, even if done by a friend, Marshal,' said Stanley Baker, a cohort of the deceased banker. Al Blake bristled at the slur that he would ignore murder because it was Dan Chantry who was the murderer. But, again, he could understand the reason for it. 'Murder can't go unpunished,' Baker proclaimed.

'My time as a lawman is done,' Blake replied. 'I'd already told you so. I'm heading back East to settle with my sister Amy and her husband.' He sighed wearily. 'Something I should have done a long time ago.'

'But — '

Blake held up his hand to stymie Bell's exhortation.

'I only agreed to bring Dan Chantry back to town, Arthur.'

'Which you didn't do!' Baker charged.

'Maybe you didn't want to, Blake,' said another member of the town council, a close ally of Baker, both of whom had been friends of Charles B. Morgan, and like the late banker had taken every opportunity to enrich themselves irrespective of how cruelly

48

that enrichment affected others. 'Willie Acton says that when he wanted to hogtie Chantry, you told him not to.

'If he'd been hogtied, he'd be in jail right now, I reckon.'

Al Blake's eyes burned holes in Baker and his ally.

'If you were younger men,' he growled, 'I'd take you outside and lay in to you.'

'Stanley has a point, Blake,' said another council member of a less biased view. 'You can't deny that you and Chantry go back a long way.'

'Right to when this town was just tumbleweed and dust,' he confirmed.

'And you did spring him from jail,' Baker said spitefully. 'If you hadn't, Morgan would be alive and kicking.'

'Dan Chantry had calmed down,' Blake said in his defence, while understanding how he might also see things as Baker did from his perspective. 'In my view, jail served no purpose.'

'A marshal should uphold the law,'

49

said Baker's ally. 'Not run matters according to his . . . *view.*'

Glowering, Blake sprang off the chair he was sitting on.

'Well, now's your chance to appoint a badge-toter to suit your opinions, gents.' Al Blake stormed out of the meeting, leaving the room door shuddering on its hinges.

Arthur Bell, the newly elected town council chairman expressed his displeasure at the turn of events. 'That was darn stupid, Stanley,' he rebuked Baker, and his glare at the man who had backed him confirmed the same view of him. 'Now where are we going to find anyone to pin on Blake's badge?'

'There'll be plenty,' Baker said. 'This town's got a lot of men wearing out the seat of their trousers doing nothing.'

'Can't see any of them willing to go after Chantry,' Bell opined. 'Most men in this town have had Morgan's claws into them one time or another, and wish they had had the spit to stand up to him like Chantry did.

'When word got out that Chantry had done for Morgan last night, no one cried any tears.'

'Someone's bound to take the job,' Baker predicted.

'Arthur's probably right, Stanley.' Baker was stunned by his former ally's treachery. 'Maybe if we upped the marshal's pay,' he suggested by way of compromise, eager to close the gap between him and Baker which his comments had opened up.

'The town coffers are almost empty. We can't afford to pay another dime, gents,' was the chairman's conclusion. He stood up wearily. 'There's only one thing we can do, and that is try and persuade Al Blake to stay on long enough to bring Chantry in.'

'Chantry and Blake are peas in a pod,' Baker said. 'There's no way Blake will lead him to the gallows.'

'That's what he'd have done if he'd thrown Chantry in jail,' Arthur Bell said.

'But he didn't, Arthur,' Baker said, pointedly.

'Al Blake can't control the heavens, Stanley,' Bell countered.

'True,' Baker conceded. 'But don't you think that Chantry escaped Blake's custody too easily?' He looked round the room and was rewarded by nodding heads.

'Willie Acton says that he's never seen lightning like it before,' Bell said. 'There was nothing Al Blake could do about an act of God. I reckon that if lightning hadn't struck, Chantry would be in jail right now.'

'Blake could have taken off after Chantry when he got his wits back,' Baker pointed out. 'No great amount of time had been lost. Coming back to town has given Chantry a head start that will be nigh on impossible for Blake or any man who replaces him to close.'

'Hold on now,' Bell pleaded. 'Al Blake has served the citizens of Wolf Creek well and honestly.

'He never had to present his best friend to the hangman before,' Baker's ally put in. 'I think Blake let Chantry hightail it, Arthur.'

'Blake was a lawman who had lost a prisoner,' said Ben Rowley, a dapper bald-headed man who seldom offered a view and was, in Bell's opinion, about as useful to council business as the chair he occupied, 'his every instinct would be to pursue Chantry as quickly as he could, Arthur.'

'Makes sense to me,' Stanley Baker said.

'Instead he rides back. Doesn't make sense to me,' Rowley concluded. His opinion got whole-hearted approval.

Arthur Bell did not have a plausible counter argument, because he himself had been trying to find a reason for Al Blake's out-of-character actions.

'He'd handed in his badge before that,' Bell reminded the council feebly. 'And he only put it back on to bring Chantry in.'

'Or alert a pal to trouble coming,'

Baker said. 'If we had appointed another marshal, I figure that right now Chantry would be lolling in the town jail waiting for the hangman to come by.'

Though having an immense respect and liking for Al Blake, who had brought law to Wolf Creek when it was most needed, the chairman of the town council was finding it increasingly difficult to defend Blake's refusal to keep his badge until he brought Dan Chantry to book, although in truth he could not see Chantry as a cold-blooded killer. However, he had threatened Charles B. Morgan, and in such a temper as to warrant his detention by Blake. And now Morgan was dead.

Murdered.

'You know, maybe the first duty of the new marshal should be to sling Blake in jail,' said Stanley Baker, spitefully.

'I'll go and talk to Al Blake again,' Bell proposed.

'I figure you shouldn't waste your

breath, Arthur,' Baker's ally scoffed. 'I say we forget about courting Blake and find ourselves a new marshal.'

'Like I said — '

'We know what you said, Arthur,' Baker interjected. 'But we won't know until we try whether we can get anyone to step into Blake's shoes.'

'Even if we did, we'd be replacing an ace lawman with a lame duck,' Bell argued hotly. 'Dan Chantry might not be a man who's gun-handy, but he's a tough-as-rawhide *hombre*. And he won't be brought in by some two-bit star-packer.'

Bell let his eyes engage every other man's in the room.

'Pinning on a tin star doesn't make a marshal,' he reminded them. 'A good lawman is born. And as lawmen go, you'll travel a heck of a long trail before you'll come anywhere near finding the match of Al Blake!'

'Maybe we should let Arthur talk to Blake again.' All eyes switched to Luke Coppersmith, the owner of the once thriving Wolf Creek haulage company, but there was not much left to haul now with the town in a downward spiral. Coppersmith used words like a miser used money. So when he had something to say, it usually got the council's attention, as it did now. 'What have we got to lose?' he said, addressing Baker directly. 'Al Blake will say yes or no, simple as that.'

'He's already said no,' Baker flung back.

'What did you expect him to say, with you accusing him of being as crooked as a wriggling snake,' Coppersmith said. 'Talk to Blake, Arthur,' he urged the council chairman.

'Right now, Luke.'

The council chairman headed for the door.

'Don't we have to vote?' Baker challenged Bell, bringing the chairman up short.

Coppersmith held up his hand. 'I'm for.' He looked in turn at the other members of the council, holding them transfixed until two more raised their hands. 'Three out of five makes for a majority,' he said triumphantly.

'I'll be back in no time at all,' Arthur Bell said, leaving the room with a jaunty gait.

★　★　★

The afternoon was grey and cloudy and night came quickly, inky black as a mineshaft, there being no moon. In the last hour or so, Chantry had grown ever more edgy, and had begun to curse the cavalier and ill-prepared fashion he had ridden into the mountains, proving the old adage that a little learning was a dangerous thing.

Somewhere a twig snapped.

Chantry drew rein and stood stock-still in the darkness, trying to assess the weight that had snapped the twig — man or beast? And maybe it did not matter, because either could be equally deadly. He tried to pin-point the sound, but the accoustics of the hills and the darkness made any conclusion pure guesswork.

He waited.

There was nothing else he could do.

6

Al Blake shoved a glass and the half-empty bottle of whiskey across the table to Arthur Bell, who barely filled the bottom of the glass with the liquor. The town council chairman was not a liquor-drinking man. In all the years that Blake had known him, he could recall having seen him only once in the saloon. Bell was a family man first and last, and spent his time, outside running the general store, tending to the needs of his wife and family, three fine boys who, if they took a page out of their father's book, would grow up to be decent law-abiding citizens.

'I guess you know why I'm here, Al?'

'I know,' Blake said. 'And I've already given you my answer, Arthur. I'll be on the stage out of here day after tomorrow.' He sighed. 'I should have taken that stage a long time ago. Before

Mary passed away, drained before her time by this accursed land.'

'You're leaving unfinished business, Al,' the council chairman stated bluntly. 'Doesn't that settle badly with you?'

Blake shook his head. 'No.'

'I don't believe that. Your pride in wearing a star was too great to tarnish it at the last moment.'

Al Blake withdrew the glass from his lips, scowling. 'Tarnish it, Arthur?'

'If you pack in before Dan Chantry is behind bars, that's what folk will say, Al.'

'Then let them damn well say it!' he fumed. 'Sure, Dan was a friend of mine, the best friend a man could have. But that doesn't mean that I wouldn't apply the law to him like I would any other man.'

'You let him walk out of jail,' Bell said, but not accusingly or critically.

'A lawman often has to use his head as well as his gun and fists, Arthur. At least the sensible ones do. You know that.'

60

'I know, Al. But you have to see it like other folk will see it. They'll say that you let a friend walk free when you had grounds to hold him, based on the ferocity of his threat to Morgan.'

'Blather, that's all it was.'

'Charles B. Morgan is dead, Al. And the man who, most folk reckon, killed him, was able to do so because you let him walk free.'

'Horse-manure!' Blake exploded.

'Then prove it. Bring Chantry in. Then you can leave on that stage with your head held high and your reputation shiny new.'

Al Blake fixed a steady gaze on Bell. 'Sounds to me like you think Chantry did murder Morgan, Arthur?'

'I don't know what to think, Al,' the council chairman stated honestly. 'Sure, I'd never have thought that Dan Chantry could kill any man, even one as rotten as Charles B. Morgan. But I also know that on the odd time that Dan got riled, he was a force to be reckoned with. And with Morgan about to foreclose on his farm, his good sense might just have deserted him.'

Bell returned Blake's stare.

'And the only way we can be sure whether he did or did not, is by getting him back here for a fair trial, Al.' Blake shifted uneasily. 'And you know that to be the truth. Besides, if Dan Chantry doesn't come back or is hauled back, he'll lose his farm anyway. Stanley Baker is the new bank president. He was Morgan's disciple and, in my book, will be even more rotten than his mentor.'

Al Blake poured a stiff whiskey and sat thinking deeply as he drank, reaching a decision that pleased the council chairman.

'I guess you're talking a lot of horse sense, Arthur,' Blake said. 'I guess this *brouhaha* has to be decided one way or the other.'

'You'll bring Chantry in?'

Blake nodded. 'I'll bring Dan in, Arthur.'

Bell stood up, his gait businesslike.

'How many men will you want to ride with you?'

'None!' came Blake's stark response.

'None?' was Bell's surprised reaction.

'If I find Dan Chantry, I'll bring him back. Or we'll settle it between us there and then.'

'But — '

'That's the deal, Arthur. Take it or leave it.'

'But folk will want witnesses to what happened, Al,' the council chairman pleaded. 'They won't want any whiff of doubt.'

'Haven't I always lived up to my word?'

'Yes, you have.'

'Well, I'll damn well live up to it now. I'll haul Chantry back. Or if he's of a mind not to come back, then we'll settle it between us wherever we meet up. Or . . . '

'Or?'

'I don't pin on a star again, Arthur.'

Arthur Bell smiled. 'You drive a mighty hard bargain, Marshal. When will you leave?'

'First light.'

Bell stood up and offered his hand to Blake.

'This burg's been blessedly lucky to have had you as marshal these past twelve years, Al Blake,' he said.

★   ★   ★

Dan Chantry heard no more, which told him that the twig had not been snapped by a wild creature, because if it had been, it was mighty unlikely that the creature would have the sense to remain as still as a corpse in a tomb. The visitor would choose his own time to show himself, and there was nothing he could do but wait.

Chantry had one overriding concern, and that was that the twig-snapper would dispense with any social contact and simply ambush him.

★   ★   ★

An hour had passed. Chantry had a good fire going to frighten off any four-legged predator who might take an interest in him, and up to now it was doing the same job with the two-legged critter. A couple of minutes ago he had heard a rustle of brush to the left of him and behind where he sat drinking his coffee. Pretending that he hadn't a care in the world, he took the makings from his vest-pocket and rolled a smoke. His natural instinct had been to turn round, but he had, he hoped, maintained his relaxed pose and had not given the interloper any hint of his awareness of his presence. One thing was for sure, and that was that whoever it was, had a lightness of foot that was close to ghostly.

A fickle wind that could not decide which way to blow had sprung up. It fluttered the flames of the fire in ever changing directions, giving Chantry glimpses of his surroundings but never for long enough to make sense of what he had seen. So when the shadows danced back into the darkness, it left him feeling increasingly uneasy, because the next time they drifted back in the firelight one of those shadows might be the manifestation of whoever was watching him; so close that he felt that he could reach out and touch the interloper.

His gunhand ached from being in a state of readiness to dive for his Colt .45. Suddenly, he sensed that the tension which had been building was about to break.

★ ★ ★

Back in Wolf Creek Al Blake was tossing in bed, chasing sleep and losing out. Since Arthur Bell had left, he had become uncertain as to the wisdom of hunting down Dan Chantry, while at the same time he knew as a lawman that the council chairman had got it right in that if he quitted without resolving the issue of Chantry one way or another, his record as a lawman would be blemished, and that fact would niggle away at him.

He took pride in having been an honest marshal, and in doing the job without favour. However, this time, bringing in his oldest friend for a probable date with the hangman was the hardest task he had ever had to perform, and were he to show favour, now would be the time. But he would not. Come first light he would be in the saddle and riding, and hoping that some miracle would relieve him of the worst duty it had been his bad luck to draw.

Blake turned over and closed his eyes, hoping that he would dream of Mary and the good times they had shared with Dan Chantry.

★   ★   ★

In the mountains, Dan Chantry had no time to dream. The sound of a bullet going into a rifle breech had his full attention. He swung round, his hand dropping to his gun.

'Leave it right where it is, mister!'

He had done that anyway, surprised as he was on hearing the woman.

7

She held the rifle with the cocksureness of having done so a thousand times before, and Chantry had no doubt that were she to shoot, the bullet would go exactly where she intended it to go. The woman was tall and elegant, with a mane of red hair, tied in a pony-tail. The colour of her eyes was a complete mystery, but they had a flinty resolve that, in Chantry's opinion, hinted at a determination uncommon in Western women who were, in the main, subject to their husband's will.

However, he reckoned that this woman had her own will, and had no intention of surrendering it to any man. Her tiredness too was evident. In fact she looked all in.

'The coffee ain't bad,' Chantry said, his tone neighbourly. The woman looked longingly past him to the fire.

The mountains baked by day but froze by night. Chantry went and got his saddle blanket and offered it to her. He could see the fight she put up to resist accepting it. 'You'll catch your death if you don't.'

She reached for the blanket and wrapped it round her.

'I'll brew some fresh beans.'

'You're mighty neighbourly for a man under the threat of a rifle,' she said, suspiciously. 'Aren't you afraid that I'll pull this trigger?'

'I figure that if you wanted to shoot me, you would have done so long before now. Probably when you stepped on that twig. Like your coffee strong?'

'Strong and hot,' she replied, relaxing some. She lowered the rifle and then dropped it on the ground, when Chantry proffered a tin cup of piping-hot coffee. 'What're you doing in the mountains on your own?'

Chantry grinned.

'I might ask you the same thing.' He put more kindling on the fire and it glowed, sending a shower of sparks into the air. When they dropped to the ground he stamped them out. The mountains had long stretches of timber and scrub. One spark could start a raging inferno. Unlikely at present, because of the storm, but he saw no point in taking a risk. Task completed, he invited: 'Come sit near the fire. It's a good fire, but its heat won't reach all the way to you. In your own time,' he said, when she was obviously uneasy with the intimacy of sharing a fireside with him, Chantry hunkered down. It took another ten minutes before the woman joined him. 'More coffee?' She nodded, and he poured. 'Got some biscuits and jerky.'

'Coffee's just fine.' After awhile she said, 'My horse broke a leg higher up.'

'A long and exhausting trek on foot,' he sympathized.

'Don't you want to know what I'm doing in the mountains?'

'Do you want to tell me?'

'I've got this loco husband who gets

71

bouts of gold-fever now and then.' She sighed heavily. 'There's no gold in these mountains, but when Ned gets the fever, there's no convincing him of that. Every time he's going to strike it rich,' she added bitterly, a woman at the end of her tether.

'Some men get liquor-fever. Some, woman-fever. Others gold-fever, ma'am.'

'You're the right philosopher, aren't you,' she scoffed. But the hint of a smile played on her full lips. And as the fire danced, it reflected in her green eyes. 'What fever do you have?'

'Well, I'm a well-balanced fella,' Chantry said. 'I've got a little of the first two.'

The shadow of a smile became a laugh.

'You should have been a preacher,' she opined. 'You've got words galore to fit any situation, I'd reckon.' She held out her hand to shake. 'Sarah Cleary.'

Chantry shook her hand, feeling the calluses that hard work had put there. 'Dan Chantry, Sarah.'

They drank some more coffee, and when Chantry cut himself loose from the pleasant thoughts he was having, Sarah had fallen asleep on his shoulder. He picked her up and laid her close to the fire. He then went and sat with his back to a gnarled old tree that he reckoned had been growing for at least a century.

His head full of a million thoughts, he had not expected to sleep, but he woke with the light filtering through the trees across his eyes. Sarah was already awake and had coffee brewing. He stood up and stretched to ease a throb of pain in his lower back; his awkward posture had aggravated an old knife injury he had picked up in a brawl years earlier, along the trail that had brought him to Wolf Creek, when a blackjack game had turned sour due to a crooked deck dealt by an itinerant gambler who had joined the wagon train for what he figured would be easy pickings.

'You're travelling pretty light,' Sarah observed, sipping her coffee, her observation a question wrapped up in a statement. He saw no need to enlighten her about his hurried departure from the Wolf Creek marshal's custody.

'Saw no need to overburden myself,' he replied coolly, hoping to head off any further questions. But he should have known that if Sarah Cleary had questions to ask, she would not be easily fobbed off.

'Where are you headed?'

'Do you always ask so many questions over breakfast?' This time his tone left her in no doubt that questions were not welcome.

'Sorry. Don't mean to pry.'

'Visiting a friend down near the border,' Chantry relented.

He could sense the pile of questions lining up to be asked, but she had guile enough to hold her tongue. Because asking questions of a man travelling light and fast and border-bound would not be the wisest thing to do.

He doused the fire with his coffee-dregs. It was time to make tracks. But that posed a problem for Chantry. A woman alone in the West was in constant danger. But a woman alone in terrain traversed by men of ill-repute and often no better than animals went well beyond danger. He could be hard-hearted and uncaring and leave the woman to find her own way, which would run contrary to his code of conduct. Or she could double up on his horse. And therein lay another problem, because his nag was not in the league of finest horseflesh; doubling up would overload the mare, and likely leave them both stranded.

'You'd best continue your journey,' Sarah said, sensing the drift of Chantry's mind in his fretful sizing up of the mare. 'Most of the hard work's been done for me,' she added, putting on a brave face. But there was no hiding her disappointment. 'Besides, your horse isn't in the first flush of youth, is it.'

'Maybe you'll come across that

wandering husband of yours,' he said, to salve his conscience.

Sarah Cleary sighed. 'I'm not sure if I want to, Dan. He's been a millstone round my neck for way too long. Doing what he likes without a thought for me.'

'Foolish man,' Chantry said. 'If I see him I'll tell him so.'

'You take care.' Mounted and ready to ride, no matter how doggedly he tried, Dan Chantry could no longer ignore his conscience. He shifted forward in the saddle. 'Get on board.'

'No,' Sarah said adamantly. 'I don't want to be the cause of the law catching up with you, Dan.'

'The law?' he chuckled, feigning surprise.

Sarah Cleary was not fooled.

'I don't know what you did, Dan,' she said. 'But whatever it was, I figure that it was way out of character.'

'Would you believe that I didn't do what I'm being hunted down for?' Chantry asked.

'I would,' Sarah said sincerely.

Chantry had got the answer he had been hoping to get, and he cursed silently that he had not met Sarah Cleary a long time ago. He swung his horse.

'Be seeing you, Sarah,' he said quietly.

'Maybe.'

As he rode away, Chantry kept his eyes fixed straight ahead. Because he knew that if he looked back, his will to go on would melt away like winter snow come spring.

★ ★ ★

'You think it's wise to corner Chantry on your own, Al?' Arthur Bell quizzed the Wolf Creek marshal as he came from the livery, riding one horse with a second in tow. His plan was to change horses to cover ground faster. Dan Chantry had a sizeable lead, even for a man who spent most of his time behind a horse instead of on one. If he was reading Chantry right, and he reckoned he was, Blake figured that he'd shun the regular routes to the border in favour of reaching Mexico through the mountains, and that choice, Blake reckoned, would be Dan Chantry's undoing. 'Well, Al?' Bell said impatiently, interpreting the marshal's thoughtful mood as an attempt to ignore his concerns. 'Will you take company along?'

'No,' the Wolf Creek lawman stated bluntly. 'I ride alone or I don't ride at all, Arthur!'

'We'll want proof, Marshal Blake.' Stanley Baker had joined Bell, and made no effort to hide his scepticism. 'We want Chantry back in Wolf Creek, breathing.' Then, snorting: 'Or dead, of course, will do just fine. Doesn't much matter, I guess. As long as we see him.'

Al Blake, his eyes burning with a white fury, swung round on Baker. 'Now that you're Morgan's replacement,' he barked, 'don't you have someone's pocket to put your greedy hand in?'

Incensed, Stanley Baker had a rebuke which he was finding difficult to translate in to words. Enjoying the banker's near apoplexy, Al Blake rode away, his shoulders shaking with laughter.

'This is crazy, Arthur,' Baker fumed, when at last his mouth could form speech. 'You don't honestly believe that Blake will deliver up his best friend to the gallows?'

Bell looked into the distance after Blake, riding tall and proud in the saddle. 'If Al Blake catches up with Chantry, he'll do what he's sworn to do. Of that I have no doubt.' He fixed intelligent brown eyes on Baker. 'You know what your problem is, Stanley. You're so darn crooked that you can't believe that any other man is honest!'

'How dare you!' Baker exploded.

'Oh, go stuff your head in a bucket,' Bell growled, and walked away. 'The pity is that two of Wolf Creek's most honest men have been pitted against each other.'

* ★ ★ ★

Dan Chantry drew rein on recognizing terrain which he had already ridden. 'Damn,' he swore. 'I'm going round in circles.' The mountains were a mystery that was deepening with each minute that passed. Trails petered out or wound back on themselves. 'At this rate you'll die of old age up here.' He was conscious of time lost; time during which Al Blake would be getting closer to him. Having thought it through, he knew that Blake would not be fooled into thinking that he had made a run for the border on the regular trail. Blake was a canny customer, and a good reader of men. He'd sit and ponder and come up with the right answers. In his time as marshal of Wolf Creek, a lot of men had misinterpreted the marshal's ponderous style as a sign of slow-wittedness, only to find that round the next bend in the trail he was waiting for them to show up. Sometimes Chantry had amusedly thought that Al Blake had cultivated his charade of dim-wittedness to get the edge on *hombres* who might otherwise, had he acted in a quicker fashion, have the taking of him. Surprise was one of Al Blake's key tricks, in a whole chest full of tricks.

Chantry thought about playing Blake at his own game by doubling back to pick up the regular trail south, but decided against doing so. The only one he'd surprise would probably be himself when he rode straight into Blake at some point in his back-tracking. His one chance was to find the Fatbelly Trail. And if he did not find it soon, that one chance to escape and to later prove his innocence would be lost at the end of a hangman's rope.

Chantry made his way to a ridge to check on the country below him for any sign of pursuit, and saw only empty country. Could it be that Blake had not given chase? Chantry's fleeting hope was brief. Al Blake had tossed in his badge and was leaving Wolf Creek, but knowing the calibre of man he was, he'd not cut and run while there was a loose end to be tied up. He'd be coming all right, of that Dan Chantry was certain.

'Hold it right there, mister!'

The whiplike command stopped Chantry dead in his tracks. Preoccupied with his troubles, he had ridden in to a cocked sixgun.

8

Marshal Al Blake rode at a steady pace, resisting the urge to trade safety for haste. He had reached the foothills, and from here on the trail would twist and wind, becoming increasingly dangerous as he climbed the steep slopes. The trees, except for the bald stretches where timber had been logged, would provide him with cover, but they would do exactly the same for Chantry, and that pretty much evened things up. If he had an edge, it would be that he had been mostly on horseback hunting down one desperado or another, while Dan Chantry had spent his time trying to grow crops in soil that was closer to sand than earth. Having trailed several hardcases through the mountains in his twelve years as marshal of Wolf Creek, the knowledge gained would give him an invaluable edge over Dan Chantry. It was an advantage he took no pleasure in, because there was no pleasure to be found in running to ground an old friend and delivering him up to the hangman.

It was hard for him to see Dan Chantry as the cold-blooded killer he stood accused of being, but he had made those threats against Charles B. Morgan, and there was a witness to Morgan's murder. But most damning of all was the blood-stained knife that Willie Acton had found in Chantry's saddle-bag. And, through long experience, Al Blake knew that Dan Chantry would not be the first man driven to murder out of desperation at losing all he had worked for. In fact, of all the motives for murder he had come across, the motive Chantry had for killing Charles B. Morgan was among the most common.

Funny how life panned out, he thought. A couple of years ago Chantry had almost given up on sodbusting to become his deputy. But rains had come, and promise of a good harvest had changed Chantry's mind. Of course the rains were short-lived and were followed by heat that sucked every last drop of water from the soil, leaving row after row of withered crops more akin to weeds. By then the deputy's job had been filled. But maybe it had all been for the best. Having got word from a messenger, he had ridden out of town to settle a dispute between a couple of prospectors who had a history of locking horns over the mythical riches to be found in the hills a couple of miles from town, before they started slinging lead at each other. But it had turned out to be an exercise in hoodwinkery. During his absence the Connors gang robbed the bank. Charlie Clark, his new deputy, had tried to stop the gang, but he was nowhere near the match of even the most inept rider in the Connors outfit. They tied him to a wagon and hauled him up and down the main street of Wolf Creek, until he was just a mass of bloody meat. When he reached the prospectors who were supposed to be at loggerheads, Blake found them sharing a bottle in friendship, and knew that he had been hoaxed to get him out of town. There had been only one consolation that day, and that was that it had not been Dan Chantry who had been his deputy.

Blake had tracked and killed Sonny and Billy Connors, but Ike, the eldest and meaner than both of his brothers together had wisely split with his siblings, and had sacrificed them to secure his own escape across the Rio Grande and out of a US lawman's reach. The last he had heard of Ike Connors was that he was living in Peru and still robbing banks. Someday he'd ride back across the Rio Grande, but, worse luck, he would not be around to bury him. He would be back East, living the easy life.

'Climb down from your saddle real slow, mister,' the trigger-jittery man commanded. Chantry, having done as ordered, the man added, 'Unbuckle your gunbelt and sling it here. Rifle, too.'

Not having a choice, Chantry complied.

'Turn out your pockets and your saddlebags,' the man snarled. 'And drop the contents where I can plainly see them. Then move away.'

The lanky, gaunt, unkempt and wide-eyed man, madness glinting in his eyes, examined the contents of Chantry's pockets and saddlebags and was none too pleased with what he found. 'Where're my nuggets?' he ranted.

'Nuggets?'

'The ones you gave me this for,' the man roared, pointing to an ugly gash on the left side of his head where a gun barrel had raked it.

'Not my doing, friend,' Chantry said.

'You're a damn liar!' He levelled the shaking sixgun on Chantry. 'I'm goin' to count to three. By then, if you ain't handed over them nuggets, I'll find 'em anyway when you're — '

'Like I said — '

'Shut your lyin' mouth, mister. Don't mess with me. I'll blow you clear all the way to Mex territory. Now. One . . . '

'I can't give you what I haven't got,' Chantry stated, but the man's mind was set and there was no convincing him.

'Careful now, fella,' the fever-brained man sniggered. 'I ain't none too good at 'rithmic. Sometimes, I skip two all together and go right to three.'

'Did the fella who cracked your skull creep up behind you?'

'If he hadn't I'd have killed him, wouldn't I.'

'Then if he was behind you, how the heck do you know it was me who whacked you?'

Dan Chantry could see the wheels turning in his waylayer's head, but they were mighty rusty and slow-moving.

'The man who did that to you is long gone, fella.'

The wheels ground to a halt, stopped by the man's rage. 'I don't figure so.' The man's jittery finger squeezed the trigger of the sixgun a mite too hard. The gun exploded. Its bullet flashed across Chantry's vision. 'Two,' the man cried.

★　★　★

Marshal Al Blake drew rein on hearing the crack of a shot echoing through the mountains. He tried to gauge from where the gunfire had come but, from long experience, he knew that the mountains played tricks with sound until it was near impossible to pin-point its origin. As the echo rolled away, Blake's best guess as to its source was south of where he was and higher up.

Probably close to, if not on, the Fatbelly Trail.

He fretted that Dan Chantry might have fallen victim to one of the many hardcases to be encountered in the mountains, if a man's luck was out. And Chantry's certainly was.

Concern for the man he had called friend for a long time brought home to Al Blake the bitter mission which had been his lot as his final act as the marshal of Wolf Creek. What did it matter if Dan Chantry had fallen to misfortune?

Misfortune was riding his way anyway.

★   ★   ★

'Would your handle be Ned Cleary?' Chantry asked the man.

The man instantly became ten times more suspicious than he had been. 'Maybe. But if it is, how the hell do *you* know?'

'Your wife told me.'

'My wife?' Anger, fuelled by jealousy now outweighed suspicion, and Chantry wondered if he had only made his situation even more perilous. 'Now where might you have crossed paths with my wife, mister. And,' he drew a bead on Chantry, 'your answer better be one I'd want to hear.'

Dan Chantry had unwisely added a problem to a problem. If he was to say that he spent the night with Sarah, he had no doubt that Cleary would instantly blast him into kingdom come, without asking any further questions.

'Crossed paths with her yesterday,' Chantry said, giving the impression of having met Sarah Cleary at a more innocent time than night. 'She's been combing these rocks, worried out of her pretty head looking for you.'

'I told her stay at home!' Cleary groused. 'The mountains ain't no place for a woman.'

'Aren't you even a little grateful that she worries about you?' Chantry berated Ned Cleary.

'Ain't nothin' to worry 'bout.' He studied Dan Chantry closely. 'How come Sarah met up with you, fella?'

'Her horse broke a leg, and she was

making her way down on foot.' Chantry no sooner had spoken, than he knew that he was in even deeper trouble. By now, due to his witless gibbering, he was, he figured, only seconds away from hearing Gabriel's horn.

'You left her alone in the mountains without a horse?' Anger, full-blown, was back in Ned Cleary's eyes. 'What kinda critter are ya!'

'I needed to move fast. Sarah understood that.'

'I don't. And I'm holding the darn gun. You parley with God? 'Cause if you do, you've got one second flat to persuade him to let you pass through the pearly gates, mister.'

'Ned!'

Cleary swung round on hearing Sarah Cleary. Dan Chantry lost no time in taking advantage of the distraction to swing a boot at Cleary's gunhand. The sixgun was tossed in the air and came down closer to Chantry than to Cleary. Recovering quickly, Cleary kicked out at Chantry's legs and whipped them from under him, sending him crashing heavily to the ground. By the time Chantry got his wind back, he was right back to where he had started.

'You ain't very good at this kinda thing, are ya?' Ned Cleary sneered. 'Stand up. Can't shoot a man when he's lyin' down.'

Dan Chantry did not have to be reminded of his greenhorn status. He was a sodbuster first and foremost, and in the last couple of minutes it had become abundantly clear that he lacked the craft to outwit men like Cleary.

'Stop this nonsense, Ned!' Sarah commanded her husband.

'It ain't no nonsense, Sarah, honey,' he proclaimed, and proudly added, 'I found me gold like I said I would. But this *hombre* bushwhacked me and stole it.'

'Gold, huh?'

Sarah's voice reeked of scepticism.

'Sure did, too!' Cleary declared. 'Three of the biggest nuggets I ever seen, woman.' Sarah, struck by her husband's adamancy, looked at him with new interest. 'And where they were, there'll be more, honey. But first,' he glared malevolently at Chantry, 'I aim to drill this bastard if he don't hand over my nuggets right now.'

'When were they stolen from you, Ned?'

'Last night.'

Dan Chantry held his breath, knowing that his troubles would only be starting if Sarah Cleary said what he thought she would say.

He was right.

'Mr Chantry and I spent the night together, Ned.'

'The night together!' Cleary bellowed. He swung round on Chantry. 'You didn't say nothin' 'bout spendin' the night with my wife. Shootin' is too easy for you. I'm goin' to cut you in to little pieces.' He swung back on Sarah. 'Did he — '

'No, Ned. He didn't. In fact Mr Chantry was the perfect gentleman.'

'You expect me to believe that,' Cleary roared. 'A woman like you, and you're sayin' he never laid a finger on ya?'

'That's the truth, Ned.'

'Well now, either you're lyin', wife. Or this fella ain't got tackle that feels kindly towards a woman.' He studied Chantry, and decided. 'I don't believe it's the second reason. So — '

'Like I said, Ned,' Sarah Cleary said, annoyed at being doubted. 'Mr Chantry was — '

'I know. The perfect gentleman. You shouldn't be in the darn mountains an'way, Sarah. Ain't safe.'

'I wouldn't be if you were at home where you're suppose to be,' Sarah flung back. 'Instead of taking off chasin' a fool's dream, Ned Cleary.'

'It ain't no fool's dream. And the second this *hombre* hands over my nug — '

'I haven't got your gold,' Chantry interjected hotly. 'I didn't rob you. How could I, if I was with your wife!'

★ ★ ★

Al Blake worried that Dan Chantry was in trouble. A couple of days previously a US marshal by the name of Barney Clancy had passed through Wolf Creek and had sought his help with the topography of the mountains.

'Who're you hunting?' Blake had enquired.

'The Hannon bunch. Wanted for robbing the bank over in Wiley Falls a couple of weeks ago. Shot down the bank-teller and three customers.' The lawman's face had hardened to granite before he delivered his next item of news. 'Murdered the sheriff, too.'

'You're hunting down the Hannon gang?' Al Blake checked. 'On your ownsome? Last I heard, there's up to eight riders in the Hannon outfit. They're lousy odds, Marshal. Besides, it would be my guess that they're probably lying low in Mexico by now.'

'Maybe not,' Clancy grunted. 'The Hannon outfit won't be expecting the law to be on their tail that quick. I just happened to drop by to visit Wiley Falls the day after the gang had robbed the bank. Therefore, I'm hoping that they'll dally along the way, seeing that there was no law in Wiley Falls to give chase.'

'Didn't a posse give chase?'

'No,' the US marshal said bitterly. 'Everyone buried their heads in the sand. Tom Hannon has a woman near the border he likes to visit when he's around that neck of the woods. She has two sisters who are every bit as obliging. I'm hoping that the gang will hole up there for a spell of pleasure, before they cross the Rio Grande.'

'You might say that it's none of my business, Marshal,' Blake said. 'But I reckon that it's only a man with a hole in the head who would go hunting down the Hannon gang alone.'

'You got that right.'

Barney Clancy's answer surprised Blake. 'Then why do it?' was the inevitable question.

'Because the name of the Wiley Falls sheriff was Ed Clancy. My older brother.'

'Tough break.'

'That's who I was visiting. Used to be a US badge-toter like me, but the long trails got too long a couple of years ago. He was about to toss in his badge but, being a lawman, the kind who has it in his blood, I figured sitting on a porch rocker would be a slow death for Ed, so I persuaded him to wear the Wiley Falls badge. A quiet backwater whose biggest trouble was a bust-up in the saloon on a Saturday night.'

His face became bitter.

'The ideal place for a man to wait out his time, I figured. Wrong, as it's turned out. He had only two more weeks to pension. So, you see, Marshal Blake. I've got to settle with Hannon and his hardcases, if I'm ever to shake off Ed Clancy's ghost.'

He looked hard at Al Blake.

'Ike Connors was riding with Hannon, so folk say. I hear you tracked and killed his brothers a couple of years ago?'

'I did.'

'Ike slipped the loop though?'

Blake nodded. 'Last I heard, he was robbing banks in Peru.'

'They all return to their roots sooner or later, Blake,' Clancy said. 'Now, I'd like to pick your brains, especially about the mountains and what they call the Fatbelly Trail.'

'I'll draw you a map, Marshal,' said the Wolf Creek lawman.

'Obliged, Marshal Blake.'

Now, as the echo of the shot that had filled the mountains faded into the distance, Al Blake hoped and prayed that Dan Chantry had not crossed paths with the Hannon outfit.

9

'Holster that gun and stop this nonsense, Ned,' Sarah Cleary ordered her husband, and added vehemently when Cleary was reluctant to do so, 'Well, do it. Before I lay my tongue on you like a bullwhip!'

Dan Chantry chuckled.

'What the hell are you laughin' at, mister!' Cleary fumed.

'And you behave yourself, too, Mr Chantry,' Sarah commanded.

Chantry looked sheepish. Now it was Ned Cleary's turn to laugh. The laughter eased the tension between them, finding a common bond in dealing with a woman who would, as she had promised, lay her tongue on them like a bullwhip.

'You know, I'm not sure I blame you for taking off in to the mountains, Ned,' Chantry said, on seeing Sarah Cleary's fierce scowl.

Cleary was about to join in Chantry's joshing of his wife, until she turned a steady gaze on him that had him swallowing hard. Instead he said, 'You sure you ain't got my nuggets, Chantry?'

'Don't start that again!' Sarah rebuked her husband. She looked around. 'Where's your horse,' she questioned Cleary.

'The critter who stole my gold, stole my nag too, Sarah.'

Sarah shook her head woefully. 'I swear a baby in swaddling would be easier to care for than you, Ned Cleary. Why I bother, I'll never know.'

It was what Dan Chantry was wondering also. On the face of it, the wandering dreamer that Cleary was, compared to the hard-headed and practical Sarah, made them an ill-matched pair. But then he had seen many ill-matched couples in the West. Most marriages sprang out of need and not compatibility or love. A woman found herself alone and sometimes took a man for the sake of protection more than out of any feelings for him. And, likewise, a man needed a woman to wash, cook and sew, and do the chores around the farm or ranch.

Most marriages in the West were contractual rather than romantic. Some worked well, but most were a matter of sufferance, because there was no other way to get by. Looking at the statuesque and beautiful Sarah Cleary alongside her weedy and wingeing mate, necessity of partnership was the only possible reason that Chantry could come up with for their union.

For himself, when, after Mary Fitzgerald married Al Blake, no woman he cared enough about happened along he had chosen bachelorhood, rather that live with a woman who was nothing more than an unpaid servant.

'He's got a horse, Sarah,' Cleary said slyly. 'And I've got a gun.' Sarah's look at her husband was one of utter disappointment and no small measure of contemptuous despair. 'Damn it, woman, we need a nag to get out of these mountains,' he argued angrily, on seeing Sarah's reaction.

'Maybe it will teach you not to take off too soon again,' Sarah flung back. 'Though I doubt it!'

'My lungs ain't too good,' Cleary complained.

'If you took in more of God's clean air rather than rummaging round in caves and holes all the time looking for what you're never going to find in any great measure, they wouldn't be,' Sarah said unsympathetically. She addressed Chantry, 'Gather up your belongings and be on your way, Mr Chantry.'

Dan Chantry tipped his hat. 'Ma'am.' He retrieved his belongings, acutely aware of Ned Cleary's brooding mood. Sarah kept a close eye on her husband, obviously fearful that he would act rashly and murderously. Mounted, Chantry rode away at a sideways angle to Ned Cleary, one hand holding the reins and the other ready to draw the sixgun he'd just buckled back on; a gun still bearing the sheen of its newness, because of the little use it had got in the two years since he had bought it, at a time when he had almost taken on the role of being Al Blake's deputy.

'Give me the gun, Ned,' Sarah demanded.

'I ain't plannin' on usin' it, Sarah,' he answered.

'I'll still take it,' she said, holding out her hand. After a moment, when his glance went between Sarah and Chantry, his shoulders slumped and he handed over the sixgun to Sarah.

'Travel safely, Mr Chantry,' she said.

Ned Cleary sat disconsolately on a boulder and Chantry, figuring that the danger was past, turned to ride away. Seizing on the false sense of security which his play-acting had given Chantry, Cleary grabbed a rock and slung it at him. It was a wild gamble, because the distance to bridge was sizeable. When the rock struck Chantry on the back of the head and he tumbled from the saddle, Cleary danced a wild jig.

'We've got ourselves a horse, Sarah,' he yelled.

'What kind of man are you?' Sarah said with raking contempt.

'The kinda man who looks after his own needs, that's the kind of man I am. And when we get home, I reckon we'll have a long gab about what you and this fella Chantry got up to that makes you so concerned 'bout his well-bein'.'

'Maybe I just won't go home this time, Ned.'

'We can talk 'bout that when we're on board Chantry's horse, wife,' he said, his humour vipermean. Cleary hurried away, drawing a hunting knife from his boot.

'What's that for?' Sarah questioned him.

'When we're on board that horse, we don't want to have to spend the time checking on who might be behind us.'

'You're going to kill him?' Sarah asked in disbelief.

'No other way to be safe, I reckon.' He quickened his pace, eager to reach

Chantry before he came fully to. He was only feet away from Chantry when the cocking of the sixgun which Sarah had, brought her husband up short. He turned slowly, his eyes pools of near insane anger.

'I'll not tolerate cold-blooded murder, Ned,' she warned him.

'Well, in that case, you're goin' to have to shoot me,' he growled. 'Are you ready for that, Sarah,' he taunted her. 'Ain't easy pullin' that trigger, woman.' He began to walk towards her. 'Well, woman, ya got it in ya?'

'Don't come any nearer, Ned,' Sarah pleaded. 'I don't want to have to kill you.'

He paused, openly sneering, yet suddenly unsure of himself.

'Ain't it somethin',' he snorted. 'Willin' to murder your husband for saddle-trash.'

The exchange between Ned Cleary and his wife was coming to Dan Chantry from, it seemed, inside a tin bucket, competing for attention with the clanging bell inside his head. The world, as he was seeing it, had tilted at an impossible angle, and the trees around him were threatening to close in, seemingly intent on smothering him. His immediate impulse was to jump up, but he still had sense enough to know that should he, he would undoubtedly topple over and end up more confused and groggy than he already was. A couple of seconds more would make a huge difference. But had he those seconds? Would Sarah Cleary continue to be his protector? She might be disillusioned with her husband, but he was still her husband, and he was just a stranger who had happened to cross her path. Forced to make a choice, her determination could easily slip.

'Now, Sarah,' Ned Cleary said. 'I'm going to come real close and you're goin' to hand over that gun to me. Understand?'

Dan Chantry's head was clearing fast now, and the scene before him came into sharper focus. Ned Cleary was walking towards his wife, hand held out to receive the pistol she held; a pistol that was now shaking dangerously. On and on Cleary went, his steps growing more confident, even jaunty, the more the gap between him and Sarah narrowed. He had the advantage over Chantry of seeing what was in Sarah's face and eyes, and by his manner it would seem that he was certain he had got the upper hand. So when a bullet bit the ground in front of him, Dan Chantry and Ned Cleary were surprised men.

Ned Cleary came up short, snarling.

'I'm sorry, Ned,' Sarah said. 'Like I said, I'm not going to stand by and let you kill a man in cold blood.'

Cleary quickly overcame his surprise. Gambling, he stepped forward again.

'I don't believe you'll kill me, Sarah,' he said. 'Pullin' that trigger to scare a fella is a long way off pullin' it to kill a man.'

By now Dan Chantry's wits and clarity of vision had returned, and he saw that Cleary had called it right. There was no way that Sarah Cleary could pull the trigger of the .45 if it meant a bullet ripping into her husband. In fact, into any man, Chantry reckoned.

He sprang up.

The flash of surprise in Sarah's eyes alerted Ned Cleary to the danger behind him. He spun round to find Chantry bearing down on him, covering the ground between them in great loping strides. Cleary, brandishing the hunting-knife he had planned on slitting Chantry's throat with, forced him to pull back from the lunge he was about to make.

'I'll rip your innards out!' Cleary boasted, as the two men circled each other, Sarah watching, helpless to do anything to stop the dance of death, as first Chantry tried to find a chink in Cleary's defences, and then while Cleary countered, pulling back to avoid the slashing blade. Off balance, Dan Chantry stumbled and toppled back, fighting to stay on his feet with legs that were intent on becoming tangled.

Sensing a quick kill, Ned Cleary charged Chantry.

Chantry went down on his back. Cleary leaped through the air, the hunting-knife poised to plunge into him to its hilt. Sarah Cleary screamed.

Dan Chantry knew that he was a dead man if he could not somehow deflect Ned Cleary's attack.

10

Marshal Al Blake was making haste slowly, his eyes scanning every inch of the twisting trail from the relatively bald lower hills to the thickly clad tree-covered higher slopes, where he reckoned danger would come from if the gunshot he had heard a short time before was trouble, and that was the way he would have to figure, in country where blasting guns usually meant trouble. Of course it could be something as innocent as a man shooting a wild critter that had left him with no alternative. Or the action of a fool, ignorant of the result of his stupidity, not understanding that gunfire in the mountains would make stealthily travelling *hombres* nervous. Any man using a gun in the mountains would risk the chance of someone being made curious enough to seek out its source to confirm the reason for its use and to snuff out any threat there might be.

Upwards the Wolf Creek marshal rode, haunted by a feeling of eyes on him. Though there was no sign that he could see of another soul, Blake could not rid himself of the feeling a fly might have in the vicinity of a spider's web.

$$\star \quad \star \quad \star$$

Dan Chantry raised his legs to use as a spring-board to hoist Ned Cleary over and beyond him. Short of time to get his balance right, the ploy only half-worked and Cleary toppled on to the ground immediately behind Chantry, instead of being propelled a distance that would have allowed him to offer a stiff challenge to Cleary by the time he got his wind back.

Though surprised that Chantry had had the agility and guile even to do what he had done, Cleary recovered quickly and sprang in to a crouch as Chantry came at him. However, Chantry coming at him like a runaway train, Cleary did not have time to regain the hunting-knife which he had lost his grip on when he had crashed on to the hard ground. Chantry took him full force and they slammed into a tree, the gruelling impact shared in about equal measure by the angle at which they met the tree. Ned Cleary brought up a knee into Chantry's belly and hot, stinging bile flooded his throat. In an instinctive reaction, Chantry swung a hammer-blow to the side of Cleary's head that had his eyes rolling.

'Stop it, you two!'

A bullet whined away off the trunk of the tree into which Cleary and Chantry had crashed. The suddenness of the gunfire brought both men to a standstill. Sarah Cleary had taken up a position on the slope directly above them. A curl of smoke drifted from the barrel of the pistol she held on them.

'I had him took, woman!' Ned Cleary snarled.

'You!' She waved the .45 at Chantry.

113

'Over there. And keep going until I tell you to stop.'

'Yes, ma'am,' Chantry said, walking stiffly, until she was satisfied that the distance between him and her husband was such that it could not be easily closed without her having enough time to dissuade him from further engaging her husband, should he decide to do so. 'Now, get on your horse and ride, Mr Chantry,' she ordered.

'What kinda woman are ya?' Cleary bellowed. 'Favourin' another man over your husband.'

'Sensible, I hope,' Sarah flung back.

Ned Cleary glared at Dan Chantry as he mounted up. 'We'll meet again,' be promised.

'Will you be OK, Sarah?' Chantry enquired.

'I'll be just fine, Mr Chantry. And thank you for your hospitality last night.'

'My pleasure, ma'am.'

'Well, now,' Cleary crowed, 'ain't this real cosy.'

Chantry's uneasy gaze switched between Sarah and Ned Cleary, obviously worried about her fate once he had ridden away. Cleary was in a viper humour that boded ill for her.

'Go on,' Sarah urged Chantry. 'You've lost enough time.'

'There's probably no escaping Al Blake anyway.' Chantry sighed.

'Al Blake. The Wolf Creek marshal?'

'The same gent.'

'You surely picked a tough man to tangle with,' Sarah opined.

'I didn't commit the murder I'm accused of, Sarah,' he felt compelled to explain.

'Who are you supposed to have murdered, Dan?' she enquired. 'You're no killer,' she added, with a ring of truth in her voice that meant a great deal to Dan Chantry.

'A fella by the name of Charles B. Morgan, the Wolf Creek banker. I was a fool. Morgan was foreclosing on my farm, and I threatened to kill him if he tried.

'I figure what's happened is that the real killer took advantage of my rash behaviour to dispatch Morgan, knowing that the blame would fall on me.'

'Maybe you should have waited around and had your say?' Sarah speculated.

'Maybe,' Chantry admitted reflectively. 'But I didn't reckon that anyone would be ready to listen. Morgan pretty much owned Wolf Creek, lock, stock and barrel. Those who didn't owe the bank money, were few and far between.'

'A killer, huh.' Ned Cleary's muddy eyes glowed with a new interest. Chantry could see that he was thinking about the reward that might be waiting to be collected.

'Go now,' Sarah said, also seeing what Dan Chantry was seeing in her husband's eyes. 'I wish you luck.'

Chantry's shoulders sagged. 'I'll surely need a good helping.' He swung his horse. 'By the way, can you point me towards the Fatbelly Trail?'

Sarah pointed to higher up the

116

slopes. 'Keep going straight up,' she told him. 'You'll come to a gully. It looks like a dead end. But right at the end, if you look really careful, you'll see a way through, barely wide enough for a horse. On the other side is the beginning of the Fatbelly Trail.'

'Now what in tarnation did you want to tell him that for?' Cleary groused. 'Ya could've let him wander round these hills 'til he's a damn skeleton!'

'Good luck, Mr Chantry,' Sarah said.

'Good luck, Mr Chantry,' Cleary mimicked.

'Thanks, Sarah. Wish we had met under more hospitable circumstances.'

Dan Chantry rode away.

★　★　★

Lower down the slopes, Marshal Al Blake had drawn rein again, this time more successful in pin-pointing the latest shot echoing away. It was, he reckoned, directly above him and not too far above him at that. The space between the shots puzzled him. They were too far apart and too few to be the exchanges in a gun battle. Before going on, he changed horses; a fresh mount would have more stamina for the steeper route he was going to take than the one he had planned on taking. A short way on, Blake spotted a rider crossing a bald patch of hill, and he recognized the familiar saddle-gait of Dan Chantry.

Sensing eyes on him, Chantry turned in his saddle, saw Al Blake, and made for the cover of the trees at the other side of the bald patch, being at mid-point with an equal distance to go back as well as forward.

Blake whipped a Winchester from his saddle scabbard and immediately had Chantry in his sights.

11

It took Chantry at least thirty seconds to make it to cover, for twenty-five of which Al Blake had him in his rifle sights. But he had not fired, lying to himself that he would not have hit a moving target, and that the distance was against success. He lowered the Winchester, reckoning that if he wanted to he could come up with another hundred reasons for not shooting. But he did not waste time fooling himself. He had not fired, not because he was afraid he'd miss. He had not fired because he was fearful that he would bring Dan Chantry down.

'*You can't honestly believe that Al Blake will deliver up his best friend to the gallows.*'

Stanley Baker's words as he rode out of Wolf Creek echoed in Al Blake's head. On hearing them, he had dismissed Baker's concerns out of hand, telling himself he was a lawman first and Dan Chantry's friend second. And he had believed that to be an indisputable fact right up to the second he had Chantry in his sights.

Now more than anything he wanted to quit his pursuit and leave the next man to wear the marshal's badge to track Chantry down. But he thought back to the days when he had first pinned on a lawman's badge, and he had vowed that for as long as he wore it, he would enforce the law whether the wrongdoer was friend or foe.

His job was to bring Chantry back to answer the charges laid against him, unlikely as they seemed. It was not for him to act as judge and jury.

'Damn!' he swore.

Al Blake shoved the Winchester back into its saddle scabbard and, grim-faced, continued upwards. Obviously, Chantry's destination was the Fatbelly Trail, and once he reached it his pace would quicken. However, this was where his superior knowledge of the mountains would give him the edge. Chantry was taking the direct route to the Fatbelly Trail, but there was another less well-known trail that would cut Blake's time in half. If he picked up his pace, he would be waiting for Chantry when he put in an appearance on the Fatbelly Trail.

★ ★ ★

Chantry reached the cover of the trees, at a loss to understand how he had. He knew Al Blake's proficiency with a rifle, so why had he not picked him off? It could only be because of their long friendship, he concluded. However, looking down from the cover of the trees at the Wolf Creek marshal's dogged pursuit he knew that Blake had hesitated only once, and he would not repeat his act of generosity.

He swung his horse and made tracks as fast as he could for the Fatbelly Trail.

121

* * *

Ned Cleary had witnessed Blake's hesitation and was curious as to why the lawman had not picked Chantry off. He could not be certain that the pursuing rider was a lawman, but he guessed that the glint of sunlight reflected from his shirt front was the reflection of the sun on a lawman's badge. He could not see Chantry higher up, but he figured that the badge-toter had spotted Chantry crossing the stretch of rocky, treeless terrain which led to the Fatbelly Trail. The lawman had obviously had Chantry in his rifle sights long enough to have nailed him, or at least to have slowed him to make it easier to catch up. 'Interestin',' he murmured. And what interested him even more than the marshal's curious behaviour, was the horse the lawman had in tow. A horse would make it easier for him to return to where he had found the nuggets in the basin of a waterfall. There was the chance that more gold had been washed down by the storm from the peaks. And, of course, there was the chance that he might be able to trace the lode, if there was a lode to trace. It was more likely that the nuggets had been washed down from a worked-out claim that had come to nothing, because had it done so, gold-fever would have gripped the mountains. But, having found those nuggets, there was always the chance that there were new riches to be found.

'What's got your interest so much, Ned?'

Sarah Cleary joined her husband who was hiding behind a stout pine, craning his neck to follow whatever it was that had tweaked his curiosity. He grabbed her and dragged her behind the tree when her approach was made from such an angle that, were the lawman to glance up, he would see her.

'Keep outa sight, woman,' he rebuked her.

'What is it?' she questioned him, beginning to think that her husband's feverish activity meant more trouble coming down the line. 'Let me see!' she demanded, shaking herself free of his grasp. Trouble indeed, was her conclusion when she saw the rider coming up the trail with a horse in tow.

She shot her husband a damning glance.

'We need those horses, honey,' he said, drawing her to him. 'It's a mighty long and dangerous trek back home. And,' he drew her closer still, 'mounted, it'll make it easier to go back up to where I found those nuggets.' His eyes glinted feverishly. 'Maybe find some more. Or trace the lode.' His eyes danced with the insane fever with which men who had found gold danced.

'You'll have to kill him to get those horses, Ned,' Sarah stated bluntly.

'Kill him?' Cleary exclaimed innocently. 'I was thinking more of persuading him to part with one of those nags, honey.'

Sarah Cleary's face was full of scorn. 'Liar!'

Ned Cleary dropped his pretence of

innocence. 'A man has to do what needs doin', Sarah. Give me the gun.'

Sarah had held on to the pistol to remove her husband's temptation to backshoot Chantry as he rode away. She could now see the wisdom of her action, because Ned Cleary had a demon inside him driving him on.

'Give me the damn gun!'

'No, Ned. I've told you. I'm not going to be a party to murder.' Now that the rider had come nearer, she peered round the tree to confirm an earlier opinion she had formed. 'Besides that man you're planning to bushwhack is none other than Marshal Al Blake.'

A shadow of worry flitted across Ned Cleary's face. 'From Wolf Creek?'

'The same.'

That was a worrying development. Cleary did not know Blake by sight, but he knew him by reputation. If he were to attempt a bushwhack and failed, he'd surely pay an awful price for his treachery.

'How can ya be sure?' he quizzed Sarah.

'Passed through Wolf Creek last year on my way to visit with Ellen Bannion. Saw Blake then.'

'Ellen Bannion lives in Nelson, and that's way north of Wolf Creek. The stage would have no reason to — '

'One of the stage wheels was damaged by a rock it rolled over. The crew decided to divert to Wolf Creek for repairs, rather than face the long haul to Nelson with a wheel that could shatter.'

'You never said.'

'I figured that it was not a topic of conversation that would interest you a great deal, Ned. You never seemed to have much interest in anything but your crazy dreams of one day striking it rich.'

'Did, too,' he countered. 'I swear them three nuggets were the size o' my fist, Sarah.'

Sarah wondered, and not for the first time since she had married Ned Cleary, why she had ever tied the knot with him. He was crude where she was delicate. Vulgar where she was proper, and downright mule-headed where she always sought compromise. Acted in haste when she took time to weigh the odds. She had long ago fallen out of love, if, on reflection, she had ever been in love with Cleary. And she was only too aware of how her doubting had increased considerably in the brief, homely interlude she had shared with Dan Chantry, which had served to highlight starkly the difference between him and Ned and, more important, the mistake she had made in marrying a man so out of kilter with her own personality and manner.

Girlishly, she had taken to thinking about the kind of life she could have shared with Dan Chantry. And the fact that there was no hope of ever finding out. Because she was a woman who believed in keeping vows, and that made her dreaming all the more bitter-sweet.

'Now if I had me a nag, I could

search these mountains 'til I found the bastard who busted my skull and stole my gold,' Cleary grumbled. 'We could head east, Sarah. Live like them rich folk.' He grinned in the disarming way he could when he was at his most devilish, and his eyes twinkled coaxingly, like stars in the darkest sky. Sarah could not help but think that had he chosen a path other than chasing every rumour of gold there was, Ned Cleary could have, with little bother, been anything he wanted to be. 'Now wouldn't that be dandy, honey? Just you and me and all that money to spend.'

His grin widened, and his eyes locked with hers mesmerically. He held out his hand.

'The gun, Sarah, honey.'

Having a history of yielding to his wishes, sometimes out of wanting to, and other times to avoid conflict, she almost handed over the .45.

Almost.

'No, Ned,' she declared, her attitude uncompromising. 'It's time you started thinking of someone else but yourself all the time.'

'Give me the damn gun,' he snarled. Quickly closing the gap between them, he slapped her across the face. Shocked, she dropped the pistol into his outstretched hand. 'Better,' he growled, and returned to check Al Blake's progress. 'You keep your mouth shut, if ya know what's good for ya,' he warned Sarah, before hurrying away through the trees to get closer to the trail the Wolf Creek marshal was riding.

In that moment, Sarah Cleary knew the intensity of a hatred that she never realized was in her, and she vowed that on returning to the farm she had done her utmost to keep going while her husband went off on one wild-goose chase after another, she would pack and leave. Her future, as a woman alone in the West, would be a precarious one. But despite the inevitable hardship, it would be better than remaining under Ned Cleary's roof. And infinitely preferable to sharing his bed.

Now that the decision which had been a long time in the making had been made, Sarah felt a heavy weight lift from her shoulders, and she felt the years of living with Ned Cleary slip away to remind her of how hopeful and optimistic she had been as a young woman, starting out with a head full of romantic notions, sure that she had in Ned, a partner for life.

★ ★ ★

Dan Chantry drew rein only long enough to check on the direction Al Blake was taking, and what he saw made little sense. Blake seemed to be taking a circuitous route, when to him a direct approach seemed the more likely way of reaching him. However, knowing Blake for the shrewd and thinking man he was, Chantry reckoned that what made little sense to him made a mountain of sense to the Wolf Creek marshal.

He swung his horse and made tracks

for the Fatbelly Trail. If he found the trail without too much delay, he would have a start on Blake that would be difficult to close. Heading up the steep slope, Dan Chantry was troubled by something he could not quite get a handle on.

* * *

Ned Cleary crouched behind a boulder on the edge of the trail on which Al Blake was approaching. He would have preferred to have a rifle and be further away, should his skulking plan back-fire. But then with Blake about to pass by only feet away, what could go wrong?

* * *

Dan Chantry was covering ground fast, and feeling mighty pleased with himself. Higher up still, he briefly drew rein again and saw that the gap between him and Al Blake had widened. The nag

Blake had in tow was slowing him, and it looked as though the precaution of having a second horse to outpace him, had worked against the lawman. He was about to continue on his way, when the worry that had been gnawing at him materialized, full blown.

Al Blake had two horses, and Ned Cleary needed at least one of them!

12

Caught in a bind between continuing on and returning to try and prevent what he believed was deadly danger to his old friend, Dan Chantry knew that there was only one course of action open to him. He looked forlornly to the trail ahead, before backtracking.

As Al Blake drew near to where he was lurking, Ned Cleary put the pistol under his coat to muffle the sound of the hammer being thumbed back. He would have preferred to have readied the gun earlier to avoid the risk of Blake hearing the gun being cocked in the eerie stillness that pervaded the mountains, as if they knew that sudden death was in the neighbourhood. But sound carried and lawmen, their life often dependent on hearing the tiniest sound, had ears better trained than most. Besides, he had more than once witnessed the contrariness of prematurely primed guns to have rested easy with one. A slip in the soft undergrowth and he could have ended up with the bullet he intended for the Wolf Creek marshal in his own gut.

Al Blake sat his saddle uneasily. As far as he could see, there was no reason for his unease, and he might have dismissed his gnawing concern were it not for the horses' anxiety. In his long experience of riding dangerous and often deadly trails, he had wisely learned to heed horse-sense. He dropped his hand to the Winchester in the saddle scabbard and curled his finger round its trigger, ready to draw the weapon and start shooting, while he let his gaze drift to either side of the trail.

Ned Cleary noted the lazy drift of Blake's hand to his rifle, and knew that he had sensed his presence. Just another couple of feet to make his shot more certain and more deadly. He dared not breathe. He fought the quiver in his shooting-hand and willed it to be steady. He was about to fire when the branch of a sapling, disturbed by a bird taking flight, quivered and interrupted the clear view he had of the Wolf Creek marshal, momentarily breaking his concentration just as Sarah Cleary leaped from cover.

'Look out, Marshal Blake,' she shouted, lucky not to have already had a slug in her from Blake's rapidly drawn Winchester. 'To your left!'

'Bitch!' Ned Cleary roared, rearing up to cut loose at Sarah. But his bullet went skywards as he fell back under the lawman's lead in his chest. Sarah ran to her husband and cradled his head in her arms. 'Forgive me, Ned,' she pleaded. 'But you knew I couldn't let you kill in cold blood.'

Ned Cleary coughed and a trickle of blood ran down his chin. He grinned in the charming way that he could; the way he had that first day she had set eyes on him. 'Don't worry, honey.' He coughed. A trickle of scarlet dribbled from his lips. 'You always deserved better than me.' His eyes rolled, and the tired sigh of death escaped his lips. He went limp in her arms.

'Oh, Ned, Ned,' she wept.

★   ★   ★

On hearing the discharge of a gun, Dan Chantry froze in the saddle. A single shot, no reply, the hallmark of a successful bushwhack.

Al Blake maintained a respectful distance until Sarah came to terms of a sort with her grief. 'Your husband, ma'am?' he asked at last.

'Yes, Marshal,' she confirmed.

'My condolences. But he left me no choice.'

'Damn you for being in the mountains at this time!' Sarah ranted.

There was a long silence after that, before Blake asked, 'Why did your husband want to kill me, ma'am? That I can recall, we've never crossed paths.'

'We're on foot. He wanted your horse.'

'I had two. I wouldn't have left you stranded.'

'Do you hear that, Ned?' Sarah said sadly. 'You died for nothing.' She looked at her husband, and grief took her over.

Al Blake helped Sarah gently to her feet. 'I thank you, ma'am,' he said in a soft tone of voice.

'Al,' Dan Chantry's voice rang through the rocky vastness, its concern sharply etched in its ringing tones. 'Al, can you hear me?'

The Wolf Creek marshal shouted back, 'I hear you, Dan.'

'Good to know that you can, Al,' Chantry shouted back. 'Is there a lady called Sarah with you?'

Sarah Cleary nodded.

'There is.'

'Safe?'

'Yeah.'

Though Dan Chantry hardly knew Sarah, in fact to all intents and purposes she was a complete stranger, his sense of relief at Blake's news was immense.

'Be seeing you, Dan,' Blake hollered back.

'Maybe,' came back Chantry's response.

'No maybe about it!' was the steely message delivered back through the nooks and crannies of the rocky, tree-clad slopes.

Chantry rode away with mixed feelings. He was glad that Al Blake had survived Ned Cleary's ambush, and equally pleased that Sarah was safe. Blake had said that he would be seeing him, and he had never known the Wolf Creek lawman not to be as good as his word. He had said the same thing to a bevy of hardcases over the years, and they had come to learn the steeliness of his resolve.

When Al Blake had sworn on the Bible all those years ago to uphold the law and apply it equally to all men, he had been serious. And his actions since then had proved that to be so.

'Be seeing you, Al,' Chantry murmured wearily.

13

'You look like a man carrying a heavy burden, Marshal,' Sarah Cleary observed, when Al Blake's shoulders slumped after delivering his promise to Dan Chantry.

The Wolf Creek marshal nodded in agreement with Sarah's assessment. 'Going after Dan Chantry is a job I'd prefer not to have, ma'am,' he admitted. 'You see, some men deserve to be hunted down. But in my book, Chantry doesn't fit that mould.'

His shoulders drooped even more.

'Besides being a fine man, he's a good friend.'

'Do you believe he murdered that banker?' Sarah asked.

'How the heck do you know about that, ma'am,' Blake enquired, surprised by the extent of her knowledge.

'Dan told me.' She laughed sadly. 'We spent the night together.' Blake looked with new interest at Sarah Cleary. 'He allowed me share his fire, Marshal. My horse broke a leg higher up yesterday afternoon while I was looking for my husband.'

She held Blake's gaze.

'Well, do you think Dan Chantry murdered Charles B. Morgan?'

'No, ma'am. I don't.'

'Then why are you hunting him down?'

'I ain't a judge and jury,' Blake said. 'All I do is bring a man in to stand trial for his wrongdoing, or supposed wrongdoing. It's up to a judge and jury to decide that man's guilt.'

'Hot words like those Dan flung at Charles B. Morgan don't necessarily lead to murder, Marshal. If they did, there would not be many men left standing in this god-forsaken territory.'

'Thing is, ma'am, around Wolf Creek Dan Chantry is a man known not to issue too many threats. But when he does, he's as good as his word.'

'Which means that Dan hasn't a hope of getting a fair trial.'

'I've been thinking about that. I reckon that I'll hand Dan over to a US marshal for trial in another town, in the interest of justice being done.'

'What evidence have you got, other than Dan Chantry's threat to this banker?'

'A witness who was right there.'

Sarah was taken aback. 'A credible witness, would you say, Marshal?'

'Morgan's teller. Morgan had his throat slit. We found a bloodstained knife in Chantry's saddlebag.'

'Along with being a killer, Dan Chantry seems to have been a fool. And in my brief acquaintance with Dan, Marshal Blake, Chantry is no fool.'

'That he ain't,' the Wolf Creek lawman agreed.

'Now, if Dan returned to town to murder Charles B. Morgan, he was not acting on impulse. He had planned the banker's killing . . .'

'Go on.'

'So is it likely that he'd murder Morgan with a witness around?'

'He just might not have seen Andy Beecham,' Blake countered. 'It was close to midnight. Morgan had been visiting upstairs in the saloon, and was on his way home. At midnight, Chantry would expect to have the street to himself.'

'Chantry would have to know that Morgan was visiting the saloon.'

Blake had the answer to Sarah Cleary's hopeful argument.

'Morgan was a creature of habit. Everyone in Wolf Creek and its hinterland, knew that on Tuesday nights he visited this,' the marshal raised an eyebrow, '*lady*.'

Sarah was becoming desperate. Whatever questions she raised, Blake had the answer to make Dan Chantry blacker.

'OK. But is it likely that Dan would ride back to his farm and leave the murder weapon, with fresh blood on its blade, for anyone to find?'

'He might, ma'am,' Blake said bleakly. 'You see, Chantry would not have been aware that Andy Beecham had seen him murder Morgan. So he might just figure that he had time to clean it or get rid of the knife later.

'Morgan lived alone. Without a witness to his murder to alert the law, it would have been morning before his body was discovered. Seen in that light, Chantry might have reckoned that he had plenty of time.'

Sarah felt a keen sense of despair. Every argument she put forward in Dan Chantry's defence, Blake could easily counter, with the conviction that a jury would have no trouble in agreeing with, were the prosecution to be even half as diligent as the Wolf Creek marshal was.

'For a friend, you deliver a pretty damning indictment of Dan Chantry,' she said bitterly.

'Only stating what is, ma'am.'

'Maybe, seeing how closely involved with Dan you are, you should leave it to another lawman to bring him in, Marshal Blake.'

'Dan Chantry is my dirty linen,' Blake stated resolutely. 'So in my book it's only right and proper that I bring him before a judge and jury.'

'So what if you catch up with him?'

'*When* I catch up with him. Not *if*,' the Wolf Creek lawman stated unequivocally. He held her gaze curiously. 'Seems to me, if you don't mind my saying so, ma'am, that there's a whole pile of worry in that prospect for you.'

'Worry,' Sarah Cleary scoffed, with a careless toss of her head. 'Now where did you get that idea, Marshal Blake? Why, Dan Chantry is more or less a complete stranger to me. We only crossed paths briefly.'

'Seems Dan made quite an impression, ma'am.'

'What if he doesn't want to go back to Wolf Creek to stand trial?' Sarah asked, abandoning her pretence of not caring, because Al Blake was too shrewd a man to be fooled anyway.

'One way or another, Dan Chantry is going back to Wolf Creek,' the marshal replied, his mood dourly uncompromising.

14

Accepting that Blake would doggedly pursue him, it was imperative that Dan Chantry should waste no time in putting as much distance as possible between him and the Wolf Creek lawman. Maybe, he thought, his luck was coming good, if belatedly, when he found the beginning of the Fatbelly Trail without too much difficulty. On reaching the trail, he found it to be free of any obstruction like rockslides which could have occured during the rainstorm.

Anxious to eat up ground, he began the trail at a pacy start. He had heard tell of a narrow stretch round the rim of a canyon further on, that had claimed the lives of many men who had not shown respect for its danger. That would have to be negotiated with care, and even greater caution still because of

146

his lack of horsemanship. Sitting a saddle when there were no problems to overcome was one thing, but being on board a horse on a narrow strip on which one mistake could pitch man and beast to their deaths would not be easy. The horse, too, would sense its rider's lack of expertise, and that would pose the danger of the beast making up its own mind if there was any dithering on his part.

Rounding a bend, preoccupied with possible dangers ahead, Dan Chantry was sharply reminded of the unexpected when, right across the trail was a fallen tree over which he had to jump. Then he came up short as another tree lost its grip on the rain drenched hillside and crashed down a short distance in front of him. Reined in, the bit stretching her mouth painfully, the mare jiggered nervously, aware of how close a call it had been. 'Easy girl,' Chantry coaxed the mare, rubbing her neck to calm her. But the mare could not be fooled by his fake casualness and snorted in protest at her rider's foolish dash that could have ended in disaster for them both. Chantry knew that the mare would remember when they came to the worst part of the Fatbelly Trail — the narrow strip round the rim of the canyon. Glumly, he thought that it would make that stretch of trail now all the more precarious a passage.

★ ★ ★

Marshal Al Blake took his leave of Sarah Cleary, leaving with her the horse he had been riding in favour of the fresher mount. Before departing, he loaded Ned Cleary's body on to the spare horse for Sarah to take home for burial.

'Will you be able to manage, ma'am?' he enquired. 'This ain't easy terrain at the best of times.'

'I'll be just fine, Marshal Blake,' she assured the Wolf Creek lawman. She smiled sadly, her glance going to her dead husband. 'I've got to know every crack and crevice, every dip and rise in these mountains, searching for Ned when the fever took him over and he'd take off on yet another search for El Dorado.'

'Mind my asking how you knew who I was, ma'am?' Blake asked. 'It's been kind of bothering me.'

'Saw you on a visit to Wolf Creek a couple of months ago. I was on my way to Nelson when the stage damaged a wheel on a rock and it diverted to Wolf Creek for repairs.'

He grinned.

'That's a mystery solved.'

Blake was mounted up and ready to make tracks when Sarah asked, 'Will you kill Dan Chantry, if there's no other way, Marshal?'

Al Blake's shoulders were suddenly laden down. 'Like I said, ma'am, one way or another Dan Chantry is coming back to Wolf Creek.'

Sarah Cleary's heart became heavy. Dan Chantry was a stranger, so why should that be? 'You had your chance when you had Chantry in your sights when he was crossing that bare stretch a while back. Why didn't you down him then?'

Blake frowned.

'That's a darn good question — a question I don't have an answer to right now.' He tipped his hat. 'You take care, ma'am.'

Sarah watched him climb the trail at a steady pace, until he vanished into the trees above the small clearing in which she was. Her heart, already heavy with grief, was made all the heavier by the thought that, having met two men of sterling calibre (because she did not believe for a second that Dan Chantry was the killer he was reputed to be), in a short few hours both had left her life as quickly as they had entered it. Soon, she reckoned, one of those men would be dead. Because she was certain that Dan Chantry would not surrender, and Al Blake would not give up.

She took the reins of the horse Blake had given her.

'Let's go home, Ned,' she said, wishing that she could feel for her dead husband a smidgen of the respect she felt for Dan Chantry.

★ ★ ★

Blake reckoned that his best bet to cut Chantry off was on the narrow stretch of trail that ran along the rim of Ghost Canyon, and it was with this intention in mind that he again changed trails. Sarah Cleary's parting question about whether he would kill Chantry should Dan make a stand, gnawed at him. And it would, right up to the second in which the decision had to be made. He knew that when and if that time came, there would be only a sliver of a second in which to act. And, also, there were the questions raised by Sarah Cleary about the foolishness of Chantry's actions after he was supposed to have murdered Charles B. Morgan, particularly in leaving the murder weapon lying around to be found. And now that

151

Sarah had raised that apparent idiocy on Chantry's part, it got Blake thinking about how conveniently Willie Acton had found the knife, having barely set foot on the Chantry farm.

'You do the job the badge you wear obliges you to do,' Blake growled. 'And leave all the questioning to those whose job it is to reach a judgement on Dan Chantry's guilt or innocence.'

Marshal Al Blake had always done as he had just stated. However, previously he had not been hunting down a friend.

Preoccupied and concentrating on putting his doubts to rest, Blake was less conscious of his whereabouts than he normally would be. Had he been more aware, he probably would have spotted a glint of sunlight off the spurs of a man who was watching his progress with a keen interest from a ridge above him.

'Well now, if it ain't Marshal Al Blake,' Ike Connors said to the men with him, whose collective interest was elsewhere, on the fine specimen of womanhood the Wolf Creek lawman had left a short time before.

'Bengy, you reckon I should do the gentlemanly thing and console that poor woman?' asked one of the hardcases with Connors, leeringly. The man's name was Hal Black.

Bengy Hall sniggered.

'Ya know, Hal, I was thinking just now that I'm the real gent in this outfit. Me being from Georgia an' all. A real South'rn gent, that's me.'

'Ah, heck, I figure we should all,' another man, Larry Stokes, chuckled, '*help*. What d'ya reckon, Ike?'

Ike Connors did not answer, his interest at that moment was solely in Al Blake.

15

As he approached the rim of the canyon on the section of the Fatbelly Trail that would soon be barely wide enough to accomodate a single rider, the mare's earlier nervousness returned, indicating the horse's reservations about Chantry's ability to negotiate the short, treacherous passage. All in all, it would take only a couple of minutes to traverse, winding round a bulge in the hills akin to a well-fed man's girth, which had given the trail its name.

'I'm going to need your help, horse,' Dan Chantry coaxed the mare. 'What's needed right now is a great deal of horse-sense.' As if understanding, the mare looked down into the canyon and shifted slightly. 'That's my gal.'

It was not easy to trust completely to the mare's instincts, and a couple of times, as the canyon seemed to draw him into it, he had almost challenged the mare's decisions. However, as the trail began to widen out again, he was glad that he had resisted the urge to impose his will on the horse.

Having safely negotiated the perilous stretch of trail, Chantry's optimism that he would safely reach Herb Gentry's horse ranch grew. As he drew nearer to the border, there would be other dangers to look out for, like Mex bandits raiding across the Rio.

Slowly, he began to think about the problems that his arrival on Gentry's doorstep would give his old friend. He was confident that Gentry would not turn him away, but was it fair of him to ask Gentry to hide a fugitive, with all the trouble that would come the horse rancher's way if he was discovered under his roof. 'Maybe we should just keep riding for Mexico, horse,' he mumbled. The fact that he was now the kind of man he despised — an outlaw — sent Dan Chantry's spirits to their lowest yet.

* ★ ★

'She's sure pretty, Ike,' said Bengy Hall, Ike Connors' most vicious sidekick, his mood now changing from one of speculative boisterousness to one of outright lust, as he studied Sarah Cleary close up through a spyglass which the Georgian had stolen off a Union officer's body in the closing days of the war.

'Gimme that glass!'

Black snatched the spyglass from Hall. His reaction to what he saw was even keener than Hall's. 'Real pretty, Ike,' he confirmed breathlessly.

'Been a long time since I had me a woman,' Larry Stokes, the third man of the Connors trio grumbled. 'Right now I'd have me a woman with a face uglier than a mule's rear-end, Ike.'

Ike Connors remained unmoved by their pleas, which, seeing that he was not above raping when the need was on him, puzzled the gang members. Having formed only when Connors had returned from Peru a couple of months previously, they were unaware of Connors' hatred for the man who had hunted him and his brothers, killed both of his siblings and forced him to hide out in Peru, a stay in Mexico not seeming attractive or safe with only the Rio Grande between him and Al Blake.

The way Ike Connors figured, had the Wolf Creek badge-toter not driven them as hard as he had, his brothers would still be alive and he would not have had to endure an unwelcome exile.

Over the years he had stoked up a lot of hatred for the Wolf Creek marshal, and now was his chance to take his revenge. But, being only too well aware of Blake's rawhide toughness, quick-wittedness and fast draw, he would have to tread warily if he did not want to end up wormbait like his brothers, or facing another trip to Peru.

'Ike, you hearin' us?' Bengy Hall groused.

'I'm hearing you good, Bengy!' he

barked. 'The woman can wait.'

'Wait?' Hal Black protested.

'Wait for what?' Hall moaned.

'Until I even an old score, that's for what!' Connors growled, swinging around to face them, his narrowed snake-eyes dancing with a poisonous hatred. His hand dropped to his sixgun. 'Any objections?'

To Hal Black fell the responsibility of being spokesman, a task he was not easy with. Connors was loco, his moods unpredictable, switching in a second from homely *bonhomie* to Satanic ferocity.

'Sure haven't, Ike,' Black said pleasantly. 'You're the boss of this outfit. But I reckon that you understand our woman hunger, too.'

Some of the snarling tension went out of Connors. 'C'mere, fellas,' he invited. The men joined him in a crouch at the edge of the ridge to watch Al Blake. 'He's the lawman who killed my brothers and put legs under me all the way to Peru. His name is Al Blake.'

'Blake,' Hall yelped.

'The Wolf Creek badge-toter?' Hal Black questioned.

'The same, Hal,' Connors confirmed.

'I hear tell that he's one tough *hombre*, Ike,' Larry Stokes said.

'Tough as eating nails, Larry,' Ike Connors confirmed, and returned to his perusal of Blake with the keenness of a mountain cat watching prey. The trio exchanged edgy looks. Trouble they welcomed, and had stirred more than their fair share. But trouble that could be matched by even greater trouble had never been to their liking. 'And now it's time to pay that bastard lawman back in spades,' he rasped.

Shrewd as a fox, Connors knew that the men he rode with would, at the drop of a hat, hightail it if the game was not to their liking. Therefore, he offered a carrot and a stick.

'Tell you what boys,' he said generously. 'Hal can follow the woman. Snare her and keep her until we have dealt with Blake. Fair, ain't it? Then after we're done with her, we'll have us some fun with these beauties.'

Ike Connors took three gold nuggets from his vest pocket and rolled them in his palm.

'Should buy us all the pleasure we want, huh.'

'Why Hal?' Bengy Hall complained.

''Cause I said so,' the outlaw leader barked, not in a mood to be any more generous than he had been.

Driven by lust and envy, Hall was in an equally dogged mood.

'I figure we should draw straws, Ike,' he proposed.

'Or guns, maybe?' Connors flung back, fully aware that he had the beating of Hall.

The certainty of meeting Satan before he planned on doing so put a damper on Bengy Hall's lust, and he backed off.

'Smart move,' Connors crowed. 'But the next time, you go for that iron on your hip or I'll blast you anyway. Understood?'

'Sure, Ike,' Hall mumbled, his mouth full of humble-pie.

'Well, I guess I'd best mosey along,' said Hal Black, tauntingly. 'I'll try not to wear the lady out before you fellas get your turn.'

'Mount up!' Connors ordered Hall and Stokes. 'Blake knows these mountains like the lines on the palm of his hand. I don't want to lose him.'

'Where's he headed, you reckon, Ike?' Bengy Hall asked Connors enthusiastically, eager now to regain the gang-leader's goodwill.

'At a guess he's headed for that old Indian trail that joins the Fatbelly Trail, just the other side of that narrow stretch round the rim of Ghost Canyon,' Connors opined.

★ ★ ★

Dan Chantry drew rein to take a breather after the rigours of dicing with death on the rim of the canyon. He had made good time, and figured that it

161

would be difficult for Al Blake to catch him up now. That made him a whole lot easier in spirit. The last thing he wanted was to come face to face with his old friend, because he had made up his mind that rather than shamefully hang on a Wolf Creek gallows, he'd prefer to meet his Maker right where he was.

Chantry's thoughts turned to Sarah Cleary, in a way that shamed him. He had no right to be even thinking about her in the most innocent fashion, let alone having the torrid thoughts he was having. He began to wonder how different his life might have been had he met Sarah when he was not a man on the run.

'Best be moving along, horse,' he said, shaking himself free of his reverie. 'From now on decent folk will be out of bounds.'

Head hung low, his surprise was total on hearing himself being addressed.

'Howdy, Dan.'

Dan Chantry's eyes shot up to settle on Al Blake blocking the trail.

'Don't do anything foolish, now,' the Wolf Creek marshal advised, his hand drifting towards his pistol.

'I'm not going back to swing on a gallows, Al,' Chantry said bleakly.

'Maybe you won't, Dan. Swing on a gallows, that is.'

Chantry scoffed. 'I'm supposed to have murdered Wolf Creek's most prominent citizen, Al. I'm as sure to hang as the sun is sure to rise. And you know that.'

'Dan,' Blake began wearily, 'you know that this was the last thing I wanted. And you know, too, that I handed in my badge yesterday. But until a new marshal's appointed, I reckon that I still have a duty to act on behalf of the law, as was my sworn duty. And,' his face became sombrely troubled, 'that means hauling you before a judge and jury.

'But once we get back to Wolf Creek, I promise that I'll fully investigate Morgan's murder. Sarah Cleary's raised a lot of questions that need answers.'

'You crossed paths with Sarah, Al?'

'Surely did.'

'I heard shooting. Is she OK?'

'Heck, you're fretting about her as badly as she's worrying about you.' He became solemn. 'Her husband's dead, Dan. I killed him. Didn't have a choice. Tried to bushwhack me. Now, if you'll just move your hand away from that sixgun you're packing . . . ' And when Chantry did not act immediately. 'I'm pleading with you, Dan, not to try and draw on me. You haven't got a prayer of getting anywhere near your gun.'

'I know that's so, Al,' Chantry responded, heavy-shouldered. 'But if I have to meet my Maker, I'll do it here rather than at the end of a rope — a damn rope I don't deserve!'

Al Blake's heart was as heavy as lead.

'Then, if that's your decision, you draw first, Dan.'

'I don't want to kill you, Al.'

'You won't.'

'I might get lucky.'

'You're flush out of luck, too, Dan.

Now,' Al Blake's voice became granite hard, 'if you're still of a mind to try and kill me, draw your damn pistol and be done with it!'

16

'I ain't going to draw on you, Al,' Chantry said, after deliberating. 'And not because I know you have the beating of me by a long shot either.'

Al Blake sighed.

'That surely is a relief, Dan,' he admitted. ''Cause neither did I want to draw on you.' He considered his old friend. 'Let's take the long way home,' he suggested. 'We've got lots to talk about.'

Dan Chantry grinned.

'If it will keep my neck out of a noose, I'll take the longest possible way home, Al. But there's one thing I want to put straight before we start back. I didn't murder Charles B. Morgan.'

★   ★   ★

'Howdy, ma'am.'

Sarah Cleary stopped dead in her

tracks on being confronted by Hal Black.

'Hello,' she said tentatively, trying desperately not to show her rising fear.

'Your man?' he said, indicating Ned Cleary's body draped over the horse she was leading.

'Yes.'

'Accident?'

'You ask a lot of questions,' Sarah said, with false spiritedness.

Black chuckled nastily. 'I'm the curious type. You need help?'

'No.'

'Ain't friendly to refuse an offer of help. Now is it?'

'Help is only welcome if wanted,' Sarah returned.

'Well, what if I want to help anyway?' the outlaw snarled.

'I don't need or want company,' Sarah stated fiercely.

'Ain't what you need or don't need, ma'am,' Black spat, and added evilly, 'It's what I decide I want to give ya that matters.'

'Ever seen him before?'

Bengy Hall shook his head in response to Ike Connors' question about the Wolf Creek marshal's prisoner.

'I seen him,' Larry Stokes piped up. 'In Wolf Creek. Last fall, it was. 'Fore I tied up with you fellas. They was in the saloon. Real pally.'

'Well,' Ike Connors sneered, 'looks like they ain't real pally no more.'

'Heck, the way they was gabbin', seems to me they ain't real enemies neither,' Hall opined.

'Yeah, Ike,' Stokes agreed. 'Never seen no one gabbin' with a lawman 'bout to hogtie him.'

From his hiding-place, Ike Connors studied Dan Chantry with new interest. 'Wonder what that fella did to have Blake on his tail?'

'Whatever it was,' Bengy Hall said, 'hearin' what I heard about Blake, he'll pay the full price for it.'

'No, he won't,' Connors boasted. ' 'Cause in a coupla minutes from now, Blake will be winging skywards to take up playin' the harp.'

'Then we find Hal and the woman?' Bengy enquired anxiously.

'Then we find Hal and the woman,' Connors promised.

★　★　★

Sarah Cleary knew that trying to fight off the man blocking her path was not an option. However, neither was accomodating him. So she decided to call on her acting skills and womanly wiles to lure him in to thinking that she might be partial to his advances. To that end, she struck a pose that suggested such. And then, added to that pose, a smile that she hoped would fire his lust to a point that made its satisfying unstoppable, and would scatter his sense and reasoning ability. She was pleased to observe his uneasy shift in the saddle, and took it as evidence of having set her trap well.

As a final touch, Sarah brought the man's blood to a frothy boiling point. She yawned and stretched, moulding the fabric of her blouse to her form.

'Well, then, fella,' she said in a low, breathless voice, 'what have you got in mind?'

'Plenty,' said Black, sliding from his saddle.

★ ★ ★

'I'm trusting you to keep your word, Dan,' Al Blake said, having decided to make the ride back to Wolf Creek one of friends riding together, rather than of marshal and prisoner. 'I sure hope I won't regret it.'

'You won't, Al,' Chantry promised Blake.

'Now ain't that somethin', Bengy.' As they rounded the bulging rock reminiscent of a well-fed belly, from which the Fatbelly Trail had taken its name, Blake and Chantry came up short on being confronted by Ike Connors and his hard-case cohorts, cocked sixguns trained on them. 'A trustin' lawman. Didn't never cross paths with a trustin' badge-toter afore.'

'Ike Connors!' Blake growled.

'Bet ya thought just now that you was seein' a ghost, Blake,' Connors sneered. 'Rumour goin' about that I was killed in Peru, as ya can see, was just so much nonsense.' The outlaw's gaze settled on Dan Chantry. 'Now who might you be? Ya see, I like to know who I'm killin'.'

'The name's Chantry,' Dan replied.

'And what for did Blake hunt you down, mister?'

'Murder.'

Ike Connors was taken aback. 'Murder, ya say?' he checked. 'Who'd ya kill?'

'A banker,' Chantry said.

Connors laughed. 'Well, my friend, that ain't murder. Now murderin' a banker is what I'd call doin' the community a service.' His laughter faded. 'Just outa idle curiosity, what banker would that be, Mr Chantry?'

'Charles B. Morgan,' the Wolf Creek marshal informed the outlaw.

'Ya hear that, boys. Charles B. Morgan's been killed.' He returned his attention to Dan Chantry. 'Now that's what I'd call a good deed, mister.'

'What d'ya want, Connors?' Blake barked.

'Your hide of course, Marshal. Right now I ain't decided 'tween shootin' ya or dumpin' ya in the canyon. You got a preference?'

'I figure it would be kinda nice to hear all them bones breakin', Ike,' Stokes said, casting his eyes into the canyon.

'Yeah,' Connors said dreamily. 'And what 'bout the marshal's prisoner?'

'I don't reckon he's no real prisoner, Ike,' Bengy Hall opined. 'Too chummy for my likin'. I figger the marshal will let him ride free 'fore they reach Wolf Creek.'

'Me, too. So,' Ike Connors eyes narrowed and his mouth became a mere slit in a cruel face, 'why don't you

172

gents just ease your horses over to the edge of the trail.'

'I'll be damned if I'm moving an inch from right where I am, Connors,' the Wolf Creek marshal pronounced resolutely.

'That goes for me, too,' Dan Chantry added, with equal resolve.

17

'Stubborn cusses, ain't they, Bengy,' Connors grunted.

'What if we shoot the horses?' Larry Stokes suggested. 'That would be certain to pitch them into the canyon, Ike.'

'Ya know, Larry, you ain't just good-lookin',' the gang-leader complimented his murderous side-kick. 'Ya got brains under that hat. But,' Connors' look was as sly as a rattler's before striking, 'I've got me this really swell idea. What if we was to tell Mr Chantry that he could ride outa here without as much as a hair harmed. And all he'd have to do is blast Blake's head clean off his shoulders.'

'Now, that's a real entertainin' idea, Ike,' Bengy Hall chuckled.

'What ya gotta say, mister?' Connors challenged Dan Chantry. 'You got the grit? After you've done for Blake, you're welcome to ride with us, or ride out. The choice will be yours.'

'Why would he want to live like a rat, Connors?' the Wolf Creek lawman questioned. 'Dodging bullets from lawmen and bounty hunters and your own evil kind.'

'Maybe he reckons that it's better than swinging on the end of a rope, Marshal,' the gang leader flung back. ''Cause as a murderer, he's gallows bound.' He sniggered. 'And,' he spat into the canyon, 'the floor of Ghost Canyon is a long way down.'

'There's a whole pile of questions to be answered back in Wolf Creek, and when they have been, I figure that Dan Chantry will walk away a free man,' Al Blake opined.

Ike Connors settled his gaze on Chantry. 'You willin' to gamble on that happenin'? Once Blake's got you locked up, that'll be that. It's my experience that a lawman settles for what he's got, and don't stir no hornet's nest tryin' to place the blame some place else.'

Al Blake's surprise was total when Chantry said, 'The man's got a point, Al. Once I'm back in Wolf Creek, putting my neck in a noose will be fast and furious.'

'You bet, Chantry,' Connors gloated.

'Don't do this, Dan,' Blake pleaded. 'You've got a good chance of being a free man. But if you ride with Connors, your days from now on will be spent looking over your shoulder.' He fixed a contemptuous look on Connors and his cohorts. 'And not only watching for lawmen on your tail. But also for a bullet in your back.'

'I'll take my chances,' Chantry said grimly.

Al Blake shook his head in despair. 'Never took you to be the kind of fool you're being now, Dan.' The look of contempt he had shown Ike Connors intensified tenfold for Chantry. 'I should have killed you when I had the chance!'

'Toss Mr Chantry a gun, Bengy,'

Connors ordered. 'But with only one bullet in it.'

'One bullet, Ike?' Hall questioned.

'That's all he'll need,' Connors stated.

'Trusting gents you've lined yourself up with, Dan,' Al Blake commented.

Doing as instructed, Hall tossed a gun to Chantry.

'Try to understand that there's no other way for me to avoid a gallows, Al,' Chantry pleaded.

'You claim that you didn't murder Charles B. Morgan — '

'I didn't,' Chantry proclaimed.

'Well, if you weren't a killer then, you'll surely be one once you pull that trigger.'

Chantry swallowed hard, and became deeply thoughtful.

'What're ya waitin' for?' the outlaw leader barked. 'Ain't ya got it through that dumb skull of yours yet, that's it you or him, Chantry!'

Dan Chantry checked the pistol and lined up the chamber with the bullet in it and drew a bead on Al Blake's head. Ike Connors giggled in the loco way he did when the stench of blood was about to be in the air. Bengy Hall's mood was more one of curiosity, and he watched like a cat creeping up on a bird. Stokes was giggling excitedly.

'Don't do it, Dan,' Blake pleaded.

'Ain't that somethin' to see, fellas,' Ike Connors said. 'The no-quarter-given marshal of Wolf Creek beggin' for his lousy life.'

'Any last words?' Chantry enquired of the lawman.

'Shoot!' Connors roared.

'Sure will,' Chantry said.

Swinging the .45 Connors' way, he pulled the trigger. Not being a gunslick fella, Dan Chantry's bullet ended relatively harmlessly in Connors' shoulder rather than his chest, for where it was intended. Reacting swiftly to Chantry's initiative, Blake charged Bengy Hall. Taken aback by the fickle change in fortunes, the outlaw spent a second too many gaping, and handed the advantage to the Wolf Creek badge-toter. Blake engineered his horse into the tight space inside the outlaw's, putting Hall between him and the edge of the narrow trail. Just a nudge did the rest. Bengy Hall's scream echoed all the way to the bottom of the canyon.

Forced to dance his horse aside to avoid being swept over the rim with his sidekick, Ike Connors lost precious time; time in which Chantry kicked out a boot that unsaddled the outlaw and left him clutching precariously at a root protruding from the edge of the trail; a root that was way too frail to hold his weight for long; a root which was already parting from the rock from which it had sprung.

'Help me!' he wailed.

Al Blake's response was instant. He dismounted and grabbed Connors by the collar and hauled him up. Connors lay wild-eyed and panting on the ground, his eyes shooting back and forth to the long drop he had almost made.

Blake, preoccupied with his contempt for the outlaw, was slow to react to the sudden wily look in Ike Connors' eyes. Dan Chantry's reaction was swifter, but still too slow. A gun exploded. Blake clutched at his side and dropped to his knees, the blood washing out of his face and leaving behind a deathly pallor.

'Fast thinkin', Larry,' Connors complimented Stokes, who had quick-wittedly taken advantage of the confusion to leap on to the top of the fatbellied outcrop. Ike Connors went and stood over the injured marshal. 'Ya know, Marshal, I figure that Bengy is real lonely way down there,' he chuckled. 'I reckon,' he grabbed Al Blake to haul him to the edge of the canyon, 'he'll need company while he rots.'

Outraged, Dan Chantry threw caution to the wind and spurred his horse. The frightened mare charged at Connors and reared above him, hoofs beating the air before they crashed down on the outlaw to crack his skull. As Connors fell under the attack, the hoofs danced on his chest until he was blood-soaked meat.

Meanwhile, Chantry was fighting simply to remain in the saddle of the incensed mare, while at the same time trying to prevent her from doing to Al Blake what she had done to Ike Connors.

A chunk of trail loosened by the mare's frantic activity came loose and dropped into the canyon. Another sizeable section near where Blake lay on his back sagged and threatened to disintegrate. If that happened, the next time the mare's hoofs came crashing down, they would both most assuredly follow the outlaws into Ghost Canyon.

18

Sarah Cleary lay back cheekily against a tree, legs spread whorishly. Up to now her luring of Hal Black had been flawless, every movement and pose designed to fire his desire more and more until, she hoped, his lust would make him careless enough for her to act in her own defence. Sarah knew that she would only get a glimpse of an opportunity, and she had to be ready to take it or suffer the horrible attentions of the man.

Feeling dirtied, Sarah undid the buttons of her blouse, one by one. Every undone button revealed more of her silky cleavage. Hal Black cast caution aside and charged forward, his only motivation now was his pleasure.

The first scream echoing through the mountains brought the man up short. The second scream rattled him totally.

Dan Chantry leaped from the saddle and dragged the mare with him away from the rim of the canyon. The horse got its hindlegs tangled up and stumbled. As the mare tumbled on to her side, Chantry rolled away up against the outcrop of rock that gave the Fatbelly Trail its name, hoping that there would be enough space in which to curl up and avoid being crushed by the mare. His luck was in. There was inches to spare.

The mare was back on her feet almost instantly and, in her terror, galloped straight over the edge into the canyon.

'Leave the bastard right where he is!' Stokes ordered, when Chantry went to haul Blake on to firmer ground.

'The trail is crumbling,' Chantry pleaded.

'Yeah. Great, ain't it. Let's just sit and watch, huh.'

'You murdering bastard!' Chantry

flared, impotent to do anything other than obey. 'He's probably dead anyway.'

Another section of the trail vanished into the canyon.

'Mebbe.' The outlaw cackled. 'But in a coupla minutes from now he surely will be.' He drew a bead on Chantry. 'Then it'll be your turn, mister.'

★ ★ ★

Though also stunned by the men's screams, Sarah Cleary's urgency to react was the greater. She picked up a broken-off sapling from the ground and lashed out at Hal Black, catching him with a blistering swipe across the side of his head that sent him reeling back. She quickly followed through, but instinct had the outlaw pulling back from the vicious swipe of the sapling. He ducked under the sapling before Sarah could check and begin another onslaught. He grabbed the sapling and wrenched it from her. Nursing the raw weal on the side of his head and left cheek, he threw it aside. A knife appeared in his hand. 'First I'm goin' to take ya,' he sneered. 'And then I'm goin' to cut ya until ev'ry man who sees ya will puke!'

* * *

Dan Chantry's eye was caught by the slightest movement in Al Blake; he saw him look to his sixgun where it had fallen, not far away and yet too far away. Blake's eyes went to Stokes, and the message in them was clear — Chantry was to engage his attention fully to give the Wolf Creek marshal a chance to retrieve his pistol. Luckily, Stokes was positioned between them, Blake behind him and Chantry further along, dividing his attention.

'You're a yella coward!' Chantry taunted the outlaw. The outlaw reacted angrily and almost pulled the trigger of the sixgun with which he held Dan Chantry under threat. Insulting the hardcase was going to be a risky business, and Chantry was hoping that

Blake would move quickly and not leave him trading insults with the outlaw for too long. 'All blather and no guts!'

'I got plenty o' guts, mister!' Stokes bellowed furiously.

Al Blake's hand was reaching for the sixgun, but his fingers were still clutching air. Another six inches and they would reach the gun.

'I still say that you're a snivelling, no-good, rotten coward,' Chantry barked.

Stokes's face became suffused with anger, and his muddy eyes became diamond bright with hate. 'You must be real eager to die, mister,' he growled. 'Well, as soon as the lawdog slides into that canyon, I'll be mighty pleased to oblige ya.'

Blake's fingers curled round the sixgun. However, hope at this point was not as strong as it should have been. Because the shake in the marshal's hand, if he got a shot away at the outlaw, would probably put it way off the mark.

'I figure your ma was a coyote,'

Chantry sneered. 'And, looking like you do, I figure that your pa was a baboon.'

Sensing that the outlaw's anger would explode, Chantry leaped aside. He flinched as the wind of a passing bullet brushed the side of his head. Fortunately, he had jumped the right way.

Al Blake fired.

★   ★   ★

Sarah flung herself at Hal Black, seeing no point in standing still to be violated and die. Black cried out as her nails dug deep into the flesh of his face under his right eye and came away with long tendrils of flesh hanging from them. Black staggered back, clutching at his ravaged right cheek. Sarah lost no time in doing worse to the left side of his face. The outlaw dropped the knife he had threatened Sarah with, as his hands shot to his face. Driven by the fury of self-preservation, Sarah Cleary grabbed the knife and, without hesitation, rammed the blade into Black's side, first meeting resistance from a rib, before the hard-driven blade slid off the bone and plunged into the soft tissue of the outlaw's heart.

Hal Black dropped to his knees, bloodied hands clutching at Sarah. Maybe he was seeking her help, but she remained unmoved. Blood spurted from the outlaw's open mouth as he tried to suck air into lungs that were flooding. His eyes rolled wildly, the whites turning up in a vacant stare, before he fell forward, gasped, jerked from head to toe and then lay still.

Now that the danger to her had passed, overcome with the brutality of her act, Sarah Cleary fell back from the outlaw's blood-soaked body and wept bitterly. However, on hearing Al Blake's gunfire, her crying ceased, to be replaced with an overwhelming worry for Dan Chantry.

★ ★ ★

Larry Stokes screamed as the Wolf Creek marshal's bullet shattered his right hip. As he unwisely tried to turn to seek his revenge on Blake, his right leg slanted at an acute angle and he toppled from the ledge from where he had ruled the roost.

Mercilessly, Dan Chantry sprinted forward, arms upstretched to act as the springboard that pitched the outlaw into the canyon. Ears closed to this screams, Chantry went to help Blake, who had fallen into unconsciousnes, mumbling gibberish. Chantry knew there was no chance that Al Blake would survive any attempt to take him back to Wolf Creek. And that left Chantry with only one hope. He stood up and with every ounce of energy he could muster, he hollered, 'Sarah!' And he repeated his call of distress over and over again. Blake's only chance of surviving would lie in reaching the safety of the Cleary farm, and quickly.

The name echoed away in waves of sound through the mountains, but it would quickly lose its volume when it left the rocky barreness of Ghost Canyon and met with the sound-dampening timbered slopes dropping away from the canyon.

Silence came back to Dan Chantry; a desolate lonely silence that offered no hope.

★　★　★

Further down, Sarah Cleary's heart leaped when the faint sound of Dan Chantry's voice reached her, though from where was a mystery; his holler sifted through a hundred and one nooks and crannies. There was only one way she could answer Chantry. If she shouted back her voice would have to reach higher up and hold its vibrancy over the tree-lined slopes between her and Chantry. She would be wasting her time. She went and got Hal Black's rifle from its saddle scabbard. She would be playing a mighty dangerous game, the rifle could be heard by bodies she would not want for company, like the man she had just killed.

But to help Dan Chantry, she was prepared to take the risk.

She fired the rifle three times in quick succession, and hoped that the boosted volume of sound would reach Chantry. The stillness that followed the rolling sound of the gunfire filled her with a hopeless trepidation until, joyously, Dan Chantry responded. Then nothing but seeing Chantry again mattered. But now, to give continuous guidance to Chantry, she would have to repeat the gunfire at regular intervals. And all she could hope for was that there was not, between her and Chantry, a malign force that would reach her before Chantry did.

*   *   *

Chantry got Al Blake in the saddle, wincing at the marshal's anguished groans. He used Blake's lariat to secure his wrists to the saddle horn, and then trailed the rope down to do the same with Blake's ankles to the stirrups. It was a makeshift attempt to keep the slouched figure on his horse, but it was the best he could do. Slowly, he began the journey back down, pausing every now and then to try and pin-point Sarah's gunfire, hoping that the mountains were not being mischievous.

Hope and despair were his lot, as each shot from Sarah seemed to be reaching him from a different direction, all the time his concern growing keener for Al Blake as his breathing became more and more ragged and his features began to set in an expressionless wax mask.

'Don't you dare die on me now, Al Blake!' he commanded the Wolf Creek lawman.

★   ★   ★

Sarah Cleary looked at the last couple of bullets she had left. Should she shoot them or save them?

19

Sarah was still struggling with her dilemma when, above her, Dan Chantry came from the trees with a man in tow. 'Down here, Dan,' she called out, scrambling up the slope to help him. When they met she looked worriedly at Al Blake. 'He's not in a good shape, Dan? What happened?' Then she paled. 'Did you — '

'No! Al and I agreed not to shoot it out. I'd go back to Wolf Creek, and Al would nose around to try and find out who really murdered Charles B. Morgan. We were heading back down from the Fatbelly Trail when we crossed paths with the Connors gang. Ike Connors had a long-standing score to settle with Al. How far is your farm from here, Sarah?'

Sarah shook her head. 'He'll not make it, Dan. He's lost too much blood.'

'We'll make it, Sarah,' said Chantry with a steely resolve.

'No we won't. There's an old Indian, an Apache, who lives in a cabin in the foothills. We'll take him there.'

'What'll he do for him?' Chantry questioned.

'As much as any town doctor could do and probably a whole lot more. Indian medicine has secrets we don't have, Dan. I've seen that old man work miracles.'

'Then lead the way, Sarah. A miracle is surely what we need.'

★ ★ ★

'He's got to be ninety if he's a day,' Chantry said, an hour later, when they arrived at the cabin to be greeted by a shuffling old man.

'Eighty-two,' Sarah said. 'That's a lot of wisdom to be able to call on, Dan. His name is Bold Eagle.'

Bold Eagle waited impassively while they dismounted, showing not a hint of curiosity about one dead man and one badly wounded man.

'We come in peace, Bold Eagle,' Sarah said.

'Peace, white woman,' he answered.

'This man,' she pointed to the slouched Wolf Creek marshal, 'is close to death. Only your magic can help him. Will you help him, Bold Eagle?'

A great pride shone in the old man's eyes. 'Bring inside,' he said, leading the way.

Chantry undid Blake's bonds and carried him into the cabin which smelled of strange scents and potions that made the air in the cabin either pleasant or fetid depending on where you stood.

Bold Eagle pointed to a bed of straw, on which Chantry laid Blake. Sarah beckoned to Chantry to join her outside.

'Shouldn't we be keeping an eye on what he's getting up to?' he fretted.

'Blake will be just fine in Bold Eagle's care, Dan,' Sarah reassured him. 'In my time, I haven't met many men as honourable. If anyone can keep the marshal breathing, Bold Eagle can.'

Sarah Cleary was reassuring. But that did not stop Dan Chantry from pacing back and forth across the clearing in front of the cabin for the next couple of hours, before Bold Eagle beckoned from the cabin door for them to join him. The cabin was full of a foul smell that snatched Dan Chantry's breath away. He immediately went and stood over Al Blake, and discovered that the foul odour came from a green paste which the Indian had applied to Blake's wound, and which had formed a crust over the wound.

'He lives,' Bold Eagle said. 'But much weakness.' The old Apache opened his hand, and resting in his palm was the bullet he had taken from Blake's side. 'Bad medicine.'

'Very bad medicine,' Dan Chantry agreed.

'Will he live, Bold Eagle?' Sarah asked.

'A great shadow is over him,' said the old Apache. 'It will pass or take him with it soon.' He shrugged. 'We wait.'

'I'll bury Ned here, Dan,' Sarah said, later that day. 'He'll be near to the mountains where he spent most of his time searching. So his ghost won't have far to travel when the fever takes him again.'

* * *

For three days, the old Indian ministered to Al Blake, using potions, herbs, roots and balms as ancient as the land around them. Nature's remedies to man, a truly ungrateful beneficiary. Other times, he would invoke a power beyond man's understanding. By the fourth day, the combination of science and prayer began to bear fruit. Al Blake's weary eyes opened for a brief period before they closed again in sleep. He slept for over a day, and when he woke, though still weak, it became clear that the Wolf Creek lawman would not yet be crossing over to the other side.

'Howdy, friend,' he greeted Dan Chantry weakly.

'Howdy, friend,' Chantry replied.

Bold Eagle prepared a broth and Sarah fed it to Blake, whose face curled like sour milk on tasting it.

'Every last drop,' she told him.

'Yes, ma'am,' he croaked.

It took another week before Al Blake had enough strength in his legs to stand up, and a week more before he could get in the saddle.

'How can I thank the old Indian?' Chantry asked Sarah.

'Your delight at having a friend back is enough reward for him, Dan.'

Ready to return to Wolf Creek and face whatever fate had in store for him, Chantry said his goodbyes to Sarah.

'If you're ever down near the border look me up,' she invited him, not holding out much hope that he ever could or would.

'I surely will, Sarah.'

A couple of miles on in their return

trip to Wolf Creek, Al Blake drew rein. 'Get out of my sight, Dan,' he said. 'Don't want you pining for that woman, and her pining for you.'

'Appreciate the offer, Al,' Chantry said, once he had tempered his initial joy. 'But if I go to her, I want to go a free man.'

'You will be, once I tell them back in Wolf Creek that I shot you dead.'

'And the body?'

Al Blake thought for a moment. 'Went into that canyon with Ike Connors.'

Dan Chantry turned in his saddle and looked back along the trail they had come. He sighed heavily, and then pointed his horse towards Wolf Creek. 'Best make tracks, Al,' he said. 'Don't want to keep the folk in Wolf Creek waiting too long.' When Blake hung back, he said, 'It's the only way that I can have a future, Al.'

20

When they reached Wolf Creek, there was only one man about, but his yelling soon had folk streaming on to the boardwalks to witness the slow ride to the jail of Al Blake and his prisoner.

'Never figured you'd bring Chantry in, Marshal,' a man called out.

Blake glared at the man, but let the remark pass. He hitched his horse and escorted Dan Chantry into the jail and to a cell. 'Never figured that it would come to this, Dan,' he said, heavy of spirit. Then as quickly as he had locked the cell door, he opened again. 'Let's have us a whiskey first, Dan.'

'I'm not objecting, Al,' Chantry chuckled.

'And no one else had better either,' Blake said.

A crowd had gathered outside the jail, eager for any titbit of information the marshal might give them to which long legs would be added instantly until Dan Chantry would become Satan himself. On seeing the two men come laughing from the jail, and heading for the saloon, the crowd stood agog. But they quickly overcame their astonishment and hurried after Blake and Chantry.

'Pour two and leave the bottle,' the marshal instructed the barkeep.

Looking to the crowd who had poured in on Blake and Chantry's coat-tails, most of whom did not have a thirst, the barkeep bellowed, 'If you ain't suppin', you ain't stayin'.'

'Damn fool!' swore the portly figure of the town lawyer as one of the jostling crowd shoved against him, dislodged his spectacles and stood on them.

Slowly, Dan Chantry lowered the glass from his lips and muttered, 'Spectacles . . . ' Then loudly, 'Spectacles, Al! When I was in the bank, a customer complained about Andy Beecham giving him a single instead of a ten dollar bill — '

'Me,' a man called from the back of the crowd. 'And it wasn't the first time neither. Said he'd broken his specs — '

'And he couldn't see very well with the specs he was wearing,' Chantry interjected.

'That's what Beecham said,' the man confirmed.

'So if he couldn't see very well in the light of day, close up, Al — '

'How the hell could he witness you lurking round Morgan's house in pitch darkness! Let's go and ask him,' the marshal growled.

From the corner of his eye, Dan Chantry saw a figure slink out of the saloon — the figure of Willie Acton.

'Hold up,' Chantry called, but Acton took to his heels, forcing his way through the crowd. Chantry charged after him but, impeded by the crowd's reforming after Acton's rush from the saloon, the only way to nail Acton before he got to his horse was through the saloon window, head first. Chantry landed on Acton as he fled past. He hauled the winded Acton to his feet and delivered a jaw-buster that spun him like a top in to the street. Losing no time, Chantry followed through with a punishing series of blows, fuelled by his anger at the man who had supported Andy Beecham's false witness against him.

'That'll do, Dan,' Blake said, when Chantry again went to haul Willie Acton to his feet to dish out more punishment.

Acton held up his hands to indicate that he had enough.

'Talk, Acton,' Blake commanded. 'Or I'll let Chantry loose on you again.'

'Beecham did the murdering. He paid me a hundred dollars to back his story against Chantry, Marshal,' he cried. 'It was Beecham I saw hangin' round Morgan's house. When he went inside, I figured I'd wait and see what happened. Because the way Beecham was skulking, it was no ordinary visit he had in mind.

'I saw him come out and slink away. He was holdin' a knife drippin' blood; the knife I was supposed to have found in your saddlebag, Chantry. Only I put it in your saddlebag to take it back out again, like as if it had always been there.'

Chantry was incensed by Acton's treachery, and Al Blake had to fight him to stop him from thrashing Acton.

'You're off the hook for murder, Dan,' Blake counselled. 'You don't want to be back on that hook for a toerag like Acton. It's Beecham who'll have an appointment with a noose now, not you.'

Eager to please now, Willie Acton explained. 'Morgan was goin' to have Beecham slung in prison for stealin' from the bank.'

Acton's interrogation and confession was interrupted by a charging horse.

'It's Beecham,' Acton cried out.

Blake and Chantry were running for their horses to give chase, but they need not have bothered. Half-way along the street, Beecham rode straight into a parked wagon outside the general store. He flew through the air and crashed to the ground, where he lay groaning.

'Guess he's still wearing the same specs,' Al Blake chuckled. 'It'll be a relief when he won't be able to see that dangling noose when they hang him.'

* * *

It had been three months since she had got news of Dan Chantry's innocence from a travelling whiskey-drummer, and Sarah Cleary had given up on watching the horizon for sign of him. Now, when she saw the rider emerging from the noon heat haze, she casually went and picked up the rifle standing against the cabin wall. She waited, the Winchester held across her chest, plain for the incoming rider to see. She hoped that should he have any evil intentions towards her, the rifle would persuade him to ride on.

Gradually, Sarah sensed that there

was something familiar in the gait of the approaching rider, and the closer he came the faster her heart beat. But she held it just short of wildness until she could no longer keep it from leaping joyously in her breast. She set aside the rifle, and began to run towards the rider, faster and faster. And she kept running . . .

Until she was in Dan Chantry's arms.

THE END

We do hope that you have enjoyed reading this large print book.

Did you know that all of our titles are available for purchase?

We publish a wide range of high quality large print books including:
Romances, Mysteries, Classics
General Fiction
Non Fiction and Westerns

Special interest titles available in large print are:
The Little Oxford Dictionary
Music Book, Song Book
Hymn Book, Service Book

Also available from us courtesy of Oxford University Press:
Young Readers' Dictionary
(large print edition)
Young Readers' Thesaurus
(large print edition)

For further information or a free brochure, please contact us at:
Ulverscroft Large Print Books Ltd.,
The Green, Bradgate Road, Anstey,
Leicester, LE7 7FU, England.
Tel: (00 44) **0116 236 4325**
Fax: (00 44) **0116 234 0205**

Other titles in the
Linford Western Library:

DESTINATION BOOT HILL

Peter Mallett

Wayne Coulter rode with a gang until an ambush left him wounded, and he might have died if it hadn't been for Henry Mallen and his grand-daughter Julie. However, Mallen and Julie are also in trouble, and when Mallen is shot dead, Coulter takes on Julie's enemies. But when a former gang member betrays the outlaws for reward money — it means death. Gun smoke and hot lead will rage in a lethal storm to the very end . . .

TROUBLE AT TAOS

Jackson Davis

Seth Tobin rescued Ruth Simms from Crow attack, thinking that when they reached Fort Union she would be safe living with her Uncle. But as Seth heads for the Rockies, the trader Almedo and the notorious bandit leader Espinosa lust after Ruth. Soon the body count rises as the sound of guns reverberates through the mountains. Can Seth, and the wily old mountain man Dick McGhee, save Ruth from an awful fate — and reap some gold by way of reward . . . ?

SATAN'S GUN

Bill Williams

Nineteen-year-old Sam Bryson faces a conflict that will test his courage, character and faith. Raised mostly by his grandparents, Sam was made to practise with his pistol every day, except Sunday. Yet Albert Bryson's beloved wife had raised Sam to reject violence. Bryson orders Sam and his cousin, Jack, to hunt down his ranch hand's murderer, Sharkey Kelsall. Sam Bryson has no desire to kill, but soon discovers that when his own life is threatened he must protect himself.